"We have to stay close if we want to keep warm.

"Move over here if you can."

Toby did as requested. Jules managed to scoot in between his thighs so her back was against his chest. He wrapped an arm around her.

"How's your wrist?"

"Never better," he quipped.

Feeling his body against hers, along with the rise and fall of his chest, wrapped her in warmth.

Then he whispered, "Being here with you like this is more important than any wrist pain."

He said the words so low that she almost didn't hear them. Except she did. And now she wouldn't be able to erase them from her mind.

Since being this close to Toby sent heat through her body—which she desperately needed—she didn't move away. She would have under any other circumstance because those words coupled with his arm around her broke down her Toby walls, walls that had been erected out of survival mode because she couldn't lose her best friend.

ESCAPE: BIG BEND CANYON

BARB HAN

Harlequin

INTRIGUE

All my love to Brandon, Jacob and Tori, my three greatest loves. I'm proud of each and every one of you!

To Babe, my hero, for being my best friend, my greatest love and my place to call home. I love you with everything that I am.

Harlequin® INTRIGUE™

ISBN-13: 978-1-335-45732-5

Escape: Big Bend Canyon

Copyright © 2025 by Barb Han

Harlequin Enterprises ULC
22 Adelaide St. West, 41st Floor
Toronto, Ontario M5H 4E3, Canada
www.Harlequin.com

Printed in Lithuania

USA TODAY bestselling author **Barb Han** lives in north Texas with her very own hero-worthy husband, three beautiful children, a spunky golden retriever/standard poodle mix and too many books in her to-read pile. In her downtime, she plays video games and spends much of her time on or around a basketball court. She loves interacting with readers and is grateful for their support. You can reach her at barbhan.com.

Books by Barb Han

Harlequin Intrigue

Marshals of Mesa Point

Ranch Ambush
Bounty Hunted
Captured in West Texas
Escape: Big Bend Canyon

The Cowboys of Cider Creek

Rescued by the Rancher
Riding Shotgun
Trapped in Texas
Texas Scandal
Trouble in Texas
Murder in Texas

A Ree and Quint Novel

Undercover Couple
Newlywed Assignment
Eyewitness Man and Wife
Mission Honeymoon

Visit the Author Profile page at Harlequin.com.

CAST OF CHARACTERS

Julie (aka Jules) Remington—Can this US marshal find the prisoner she lost and risk losing her best friend?

Toby Ward—This US marshal survives a helicopter crash, but can he risk his heart as he searches for a dangerous felon?

Theodore the Terrible—How long can this dangerous felon avoid recapture?

Jodie Symes Benning—How well does she really know her cousin?

Chapter One

"Mayday, Mayday, Mayday."

Those were the last words US marshal Julie "Jules" Remington remembered hearing as the prison transport chopper spun out of control before slamming into the hard earth.

The Huey II that Jules and her partner, Toby Ward, had officially hitched a ride on while it was on its way to Lackland Air Force Base near San Antonio suffered a catastrophic tail-rotor failure. Their job had been to transport one of the most dangerous and elusive criminals of her tenure and deliver him in one piece to the Dominguez State Prison.

The assignment shouldn't have turned this way.

Forcing her eyes open, Jules pushed through the heavy fog wrapping long tentacles around her brain, squeezing. The scene was a blur. The chopper she'd been thrown from was smashed on its side as though it had been stomped on first, the result of a child's temper tantrum. She'd been thrown twenty feet from the chopper and, miraculously, was still alive.

The Chisos Mountains seemed to rise from the dry desert like sentinels off in the distance. The landscape beneath her was nothing more than scrub, rocks and dry dirt. She squinted, spit dust out of her mouth as rolling, dark storm clouds formed an ominous canopy overhead. Lightning split the sky in half.

And then she saw him.

Captain Crawford, the pilot, was strapped in his seat, gaze fixed, head split open. Still. His skin paled from all the blood pooling to his side after his heart had stopped beating. Eyes open, his lips parted like he was in the middle of a sentence that he would never finish. Had he been calling for help? Announcing the chopper was about to crash?

Mayday, Mayday, Mayday.

Hadn't she heard him thump the control panel and complain about static coming over the comms system?

Jules tried to lift her head up. Movement caused blinding pain. She had to push through, find the other two people who were, at present, unaccounted for.

Where was Toby? Panic caused a crushing weight on her chest. Breathing hurt.

Frantic at this point, Jules pulled on all her willpower to focus, to see. She scanned the area. Her gaze locked on to a male figure another twenty feet away, slowly stirring. *Toby!* The fact he was moving, albeit slowly, was a good sign!

Her heart practically sang. Her next immediate thought? Where was Theodore Symes, aka Theodore the Terrible or Theodore Crimes?

This bastard had eluded capture for eleven years. He was truly evil: a known rapist and murderer who "charmed" his way into a victim's life by pretending to be weakened or injured. A surveillance camera once showed him using crutches to disarm one of his victims at a gas station. The man always knew to keep his face off camera. Symes was smart.

Once captured, he'd proudly led investigators to twenty-six grave sites. He'd provided clues to what happened in at least a dozen more cases, all while smiling, clearly pleased with himself like this was a twisted game of hide-and-seek. His rampage had lasted eleven years and spanned five Southwestern states from Texas to California.

But where was he now?

A visual sweep of the area showed no other bodies in the vicinity. Had he been thrown from the chopper too? Was he behind one of the boulders? Had he managed to escape harm, roll away and disappear before anyone else broke consciousness?

To her left, the flat landscape gave her a decent view everywhere except where the chopper blocked her vision. Her last memory of flying over Big Bend National Park near the Texas-Mexico border meant they were far away from any towns.

Toby groaned. "Jules?"

"I'm here," she managed to say, though her throat felt like sandpaper and moving felt like she'd been dipped in molasses. Her hand instinctively reached for the spot on the side of her head with the most pain. Wet, tacky fingers lowered in front of her eyes. Blood.

"The captain," Toby said, grief in his tone. On his side, he managed to reposition so the two of them could look directly at each other.

"I know," she said. Her heart sank. She knew firsthand how devastating news of any kind of crash could be after the accident last month that left her beloved grandparents in a coma, let alone one that took someone's life. Captain Crawford wore a gold band on his ring finger. Someone had lost a husband and didn't know it yet. A father too? Jules's heart ached.

"Symes?" Toby asked.

She shot a look that Toby understood without words.

Right now, she had to shove all other thoughts aside to focus on locating Symes.

Movement shot lightning bolts of pain through her abdomen. A quick body scan revealed no obvious broken bones. Although, her left knee was already swelling. Since she was lying on her left side, she assumed this was the main area of impact.

Memories were blurred about what had specifically happened after *Mayday*.

"How badly are you hurt?" she asked Toby.

"I'm feeling like a punching bag," he shot back. He was talking. His sentences made sense, and he wasn't slurring his words. She'd take that as a good sign cognitive function hadn't been impaired. "How about you?"

"I'm still kicking," she said with a half-hearted smile. The sandpaper feeling in her throat made sense when she realized she'd eaten a mouthful of dust upon impact. "Symes is gone. I can't see him anywhere."

"I noticed," he said, his voice raspy. "That son of a bitch better be in worse shape is all I can say."

"A dead man can't serve time for his crimes, Toby. Symes needs to face justice for all the lives he took and the carnage he left behind."

"No argument there," Toby admitted.

Talking was draining a lot of energy. Energy she didn't have to give. Was he dead? Had he been thrown from the chopper? Was he alive?

Toby got quiet. Jules knew why. Rapists hit him harder than most criminals. She'd been afraid he might not be able to be objective when it came to Symes. So far, though, Toby had gritted his teeth, kept quiet and done the job. There was a story behind his reaction, though. One that three years of being best friends and colleagues hadn't revealed.

Asking around felt like a betrayal, so she didn't. Toby would reveal the reason in time when he was ready. Jules respected his wishes.

"Can you get up?" she asked.

"My arm is probably broken," he said, wincing in pain with movement. At six feet one inch of solid muscle, Toby was considered slightly above average in height for a Texan and far stronger. A broken arm while stranded out here wasn't good.

"How badly does it hurt?" she asked.

"It's not great, but I'll live," Toby responded. Leave it to Toby to downplay a serious injury. Right now, as difficult as it might be, she had to focus on trying to get help and finding Symes.

Clouds thickened overhead. They'd been trying to beat the storm across the desert. Lightning shot sideways across an otherwise dark sky, illuminating the scene.

Help. They needed an EMT.

Jules reached for her cell, cursed when she realized it wasn't inside the pocket of her blazer. Where could it…?

She saw it not more than five feet from her current position, shattered. The brand-new cell didn't have all the protections put in place yet, like a case and screen protector. The damn thing wouldn't do any good now.

"Do you have your cell on you?" she asked as she forced herself to sit up.

"You're bleeding," Toby said, his voice filled with concern.

"It's a scratch." From this vantage point, she could see more of the perimeter of the crash. Still no sign of Symes, dead or alive.

"That's affirmative on the cell," Toby said after he fished inside his pocket and retrieved it, then held it up.

Was Symes lying on the other side of the chopper? Waking up? Assessing his injuries too?

Symes was equal in height to Toby but no match for his muscled frame. Symes could best be described as tall with a runner's build. He had sandy-blond hair and blue eyes, along with a small scar on his chin and two others on his left cheek. *From his victims?*

The man was human garbage with blue eyes.

People always said you could tell a lot about a person from their eyes. Jules wasn't so sure she bought into that. She'd looked into the magnetic eyes of many pathological liars during her career, and thought she would probably have allowed them to carry her groceries to her car at the market if they'd asked. Working for the Marshals Service, her radar was always on. She stayed on high alert. The average person didn't live life with their guard up.

The most successful, most devious criminals gave away nothing in their eyes.

Toby might be the same height, but that was where the similarities with Symes ended. Toby's hair was almost jet-black. His cut was military short, revealing a face of hard angles. He had that whole strong-jaw bit nailed.

His eyes were the most golden shade of brown she'd ever seen, let alone stared into. Being attracted to her best friend was more than inconvenient. It was downright painful, considering there was no chance the two would ever be more than friends.

Jules watched as Toby moved his phone around in the air. No bars?

At least they'd survived the crash. She forced her thoughts away from the pilot. Compartmentalizing her emotions kept her focus sharp. They would hit once the case was over with the force of a brick wall.

In thinking about the onslaught to come, she'd never felt more alone.

"I'VE GOT NOTHING out here," Toby said as pain riddled his body. The year he'd played varsity football in high school under Friday night lights couldn't hold a candle to this agony.

"Could be the weather," Jules pointed out as she slowly inched toward him. Relief slammed into him with the force of a tsunami that she was alive. The image—which had been nothing more than a flash of Jules lying on her side with her gaze fixed—seared into his brain, shocking him awake.

He couldn't lose his best friend.

"What about you?" he asked. Sitting up required heroic effort. The scratch on her forehead was more like a gash. "You're bleeding more than you realize."

"A few of my brains may have fallen out, but I'll be okay," she said, cracking a smile. It was just like Jules to attempt to lighten the mood when she was bleeding from her head.

"If your IQ drops, you'll finally be down in my range," he shot back. Smiling hurt. Laughing hurt. But it was necessary to break the tension so they could think clearly.

"You're the smartest guy I know," she countered as she got close enough for him to assess the damage.

"Exactly," he stated with a smirk. "Operative word being *guy*. Women have always been smarter. It's about time you stopped being sexist and claimed superiority."

Jules's laugh was freakin' music. Her face was beauty. She had the doe-eyed, heart-shaped-lips thing down pat.

Those full breasts and just the right amount of curves in her hips made her perfect on a physical level. Jules was also intelligent, funny and completely unaware of her effect on the opposite sex. If she wasn't his coworker and best friend, he would have asked her out on day one. A woman like her would have shot him down, but he would have taken a chance.

Someone like Jules deserved to know how attractive she was. The words *total package* came to mind. But it wouldn't sound right coming from the guy who was securely in the friend zone.

Right now, she had decided to add playing nursemaid to her list of talents.

"I'm good," he said as he looked into concerned eyes. "I know you want to take off and find Symes. Go ahead. Don't let that bastard get away."

Rapists were the lowest of all scum. Bottom dwellers, opportunistic feeders. He clenched his back teeth so hard they might crack as a memory stomped through his thoughts. He forced it back into the shadows before the darkness consumed him.

"I'm not leaving you," Jules protested.

"I'd rather die than let this son of a bitch get away," he stated.

"He could be dead," she pointed out.

"Either way, I need confirmation." He gave her puppy eyes that she swore were irresistible. "Please. For me."

Jules issued a sharp sigh but nodded.

"When you get back, we take care of the gash on the side of your head. Deal?"

"No, sir," she argued. "Your arm takes priority. Then we'll deal with my scrape."

Arguing with a stubborn person was a waste of time, so he said, "Okay."

Jules moved a little faster now but favored her left leg. It didn't look like she was in much pain. But knowing her, she probably refused to think about it. The headache from hitting her head would take hold later. Mild shock might be masking the pain for the time being.

Later?

Toby assessed their situation. At this point, they were potentially stranded with no food, water or shelter, aside from the chopper that currently housed the pilot, rest his soul.

Comms were nada. Reaching the outside world might not be possible. Dark gray rolling clouds filled the sky, making one o'clock in the afternoon feel more like midnight. Jules was injured. He was worse off. And, at present, they didn't have a visual on Symes.

That could change at any moment. Jules would surely spot the man on the other side of the chopper if he was there. They'd crashed on a plateau. Symes might have been shot down the hill on the opposite side. Death was an easy out. The man deserved hard time in a maximum-security prison, and the families of his victims needed justice to be served.

At the very least, Symes would have minor injuries. On the other hand, he might be dead. Jules had been right about one thing, though. This bastard deserved to pay for his crimes with a life behind bars. The thought of him escaping—as minuscule as the chance might be—sent fire raging through Toby's veins. Retribution should be served on bastards like Symes.

Jules came around to the chopper. She stopped, holding herself upright with a steady hand on the Huey. The look on her face lit a fire in the pit of his stomach. He waited to hear the words he feared were about to come out of her mouth.

"I can't find him anywhere," she said, wincing in pain as she put weight on her left leg.

"He couldn't have gone far." Toby released a grunt as he forced himself to stand. Two steps later, his legs gave out and he was back on the ground. He landed hard, butt-down on the unforgiving earth. And maybe cracked his tailbone in the process.

As if the day couldn't get any worse but Mother Nature decided to prove otherwise, big splotches of rain pounded his forehead.

Toby released a string of curses that would've made his grandmother threaten to wash his mouth out with a bar of soap if she was still living.

Hell would freeze over before he would sit here while Symes was out there escaping. "Eleven years."

"I know," Jules soothed.

"At least three dozen women, probably more," he continued, the all-consuming rage threatening to boil over as those horrific memories surfaced and an old feeling of help-lessness engulfed him.

"It's awful," she said, studying him. "Worse than awful. The man is pure evil."

"We have to go after him," Toby stated matter-of-factly.

"Why don't we stay close to the chopper in case he comes back or help arrives?" she asked. Her brain had shifted into logic-mode while his was fueled by anger from the deep reaches of his soul. Considering his injuries, her sug-gestion was most likely the right move. The weather was changing fast.

Still. He couldn't let it go.

"What if a family is camping nearby?" he asked. It wasn't

impossible. Although early November wasn't the busiest time of the year for the national park, a family or couple could be taking advantage of the lull in activity.

Jules chewed on the inside of her cheek, holding back the words she wanted to speak.

"What?" he asked, able to read her like a book.

She studied him. "Let's think this through before acting irrationally."

"I've never been clearer on what needs to happen," he countered, feeling himself get riled up and hearing the frustration in his own tone.

"You sure about that?" Jules asked, cocking her head to one side.

Toby clamped his mouth shut before he said something he might regret or closed hers with a kiss.

Where the hell did that thought come from?

Chapter Two

"It's not safe to venture too far away from the chopper," Jules pointed out to Toby, treading lightly as she considered the look in his eyes. He was frustrated and angry...and something else she couldn't quite put her finger on. Rapists had always been a touchy topic for him. The thought of Symes getting away was eating him from the inside out. Understandable. Jules felt the same.

But they needed to be practical.

"Even if he did manage to crawl away with only a few scrapes, which I doubt, he won't make it far," she said. "He's in handcuffs, which will severely limit his ability to hunt for food or attack someone." She glanced up at the sky. "Plus, the weather is turning on him too."

Toby wouldn't make eye contact—a bad sign.

"We can request a search team once the storm dies down," she reasoned. "How far can he go with no food or supplies?"

Toby managed to stand up and stay on his feet on the second attempt. He moved near her, holding on to the Huey's body. There was so much pain in those honey-brown eyes of his, her heart ached.

"I promise we won't let this bastard slip away again," she said, but they both knew she was trying to infuse hope into the situation.

"We need to find him, Jules."

"I know," she agreed.

"We're responsible for this mess," Toby said as his face lost color.

"You're in too much pain to stand up, let alone go after Symes, so…"

Before she could finish her sentence, Toby swayed, and then his eyes fluttered.

He was about to lose consciousness.

Jules's quick reflexes kept her best friend's head from smacking the chopper or the ground or both. Holding Toby by his underarms as he faced her didn't last. Soon, they were both on the ground, with him on top of her.

"Hey," she said, searching his face for any signs of life. The pain must have been what took him down, because he appeared to be breathing well enough. A person could only take so much before passing out. Or maybe he struck his head on impact and would be in and out of consciousness for a while?

Rain was coming down in buckets by this point. They were both soaked, which didn't make Toby weigh any less.

Jules wriggled out from underneath him, then rolled him onto his side. Tucking him underneath the chopper as much as possible, she forced herself to stand up and check for anything she could use to make a temporary shelter.

Toby wasn't going anywhere. She'd moved him as much as she could without throwing her back out or risking injuring herself further. The knee wasn't improving. At this point, she could walk on it. How long would that last? Running would prove a challenge without a healthy dose of adrenaline to boost her.

Two fingers on Toby's wrist indicated a strong pulse.

Now it was a waiting game to see when he would open his eyes again.

In the meantime, she needed to secure the area. Symes might come back, figuring they would go looking for him or be dead. It was only conjecture, but she assumed he'd survived the crash, assessed the situation and bolted before either of them had opened their eyes. It was a wonder he'd let them live.

Unless he'd figured nature would do the trick for him, keeping his hands clean from murdering federal officers. Or Jules had stirred before Symes could finish the job the crash had started.

The man had survival skills. He'd bragged about spending weeks off the grid in Montana while law enforcement stayed a step behind. He would use anything and everything in his environment to his advantage. Jules's weapon was still strapped to her. The imprint of the shoulder holster would no doubt linger for hours, if not days.

What would Symes take from the chopper?

What was there to steal?

He would want food, but there was none. They'd had no scheduled stops. He'd been fed breakfast before takeoff. It wasn't like he would have packed a sack lunch. There were no snacks on board that Jules had been aware of.

Food and water would be his immediate need. Actually, water would be a priority. Dehydration would kill him faster than starvation.

Toby was right, though. This predator would hunt for signs of campers. He would have no qualms about murdering a family if it meant staying alive. A felon like Symes had no conscience whatsoever. Again, she wondered why he hadn't slammed a boulder into her or Toby's head or taken their weapons.

Maybe he couldn't risk either waking up?

At Symes's most base level, he was a coward, slinking off without a fair fight.

Refocusing on what she could use, she performed a mental inventory. Her cell was broken. Toby had no coverage. There was no way to study a map of the park to find the nearest water source without either phone.

Rain. Duh.

Jules realized Symes would most likely find a way to capture rainwater, which was a good idea for her too. Rescue should be soon, she hoped. But she had to prepare for the worst, meaning they might have to find a way to survive and get themselves to safety.

Bringing up her fingers to massage her temples as her head pounded, she searched the cockpit and located a thermal mug that had coffee remnants inside. She brought it out into the rain and rinsed the mouthpiece as best as she could, unscrewing the lid before swishing rain around to clean out the coffee. In her backpack, she had an alcohol wipe. She retrieved it and wiped down the rim where the pilot's lips had been.

This thermos looked to be about sixteen ounces. After setting it up on a rock to collect water on its own, she searched for anything else that might prove useful.

The headache pounding, moving in tempo with her pulse, felt like a drummer beating a drum inside her skull. Pushing through the pain, wishing she had thought to pack ibuprofen, she searched for another container to fill. It dawned on her that she'd brought a backpack with a few items. Mostly, it held her keys and wallet, along with the current book she was reading. But she recalled there was a bottle of water in there too and a spare for Toby because he always bummed a drink of hers instead of carrying one for himself.

Progress.

If Symes wasn't dead, would he have stolen one of their service weapons?

Biting her lip to keep from cursing from pain as she reached down for her backup weapon, she knew. The SIG Sauer was missing. The pain shooting down her leg kept her from noticing the weight difference on her ankle. Otherwise, she would have realized the SIG was gone sooner.

That meant Symes had enough cognitive function to think about stealing a weapon for protection. It occurred to her that he'd probably slipped the handcuff key off her or Toby while they were unconscious. He'd worked quickly.

Symes was out there somewhere on the hunt for shelter if he hadn't already found it. They were lucky he hadn't killed them. Had she interrupted him by stirring, like she'd originally thought? Based on the time when she'd checked her watch, she wasn't out for long. He might not have been either. Had he been unconscious at all?

At the very least, he had a head start. She couldn't be certain he hadn't located her phone and smashed it against a rock. At this point, anything was possible. Toby's was still intact. Symes hadn't tried anything there.

She moved to Toby and checked for his backup weapon. It was still there. Based on what she knew so far, Symes had enough presence of mind to check her for a weapon and steal her SIG.

Was that why she'd stirred when she had? Had she felt someone touching her? The thought gave her the creeps. Even more considering Symes's criminal background. An involuntary shiver rocked her. He would do a lot more than that if he had the opportunity, and she knew it.

There wasn't anything else she could use inside the Huey to cover Toby, so she took off her jacket and placed it on his torso, not that it did a whole lot of good. A cold front moved in with the rain, causing her to shiver again. She rubbed her arms. The blue button-down blouse provided very little shield from the winds that had picked up.

Could she get Toby into the back of the chopper, out of the rain?

Movement in the distance caught her eye as a figure moved toward her. The person or animal wasn't much more than a blot on the landscape at this point.

Jules drew her weapon and spread out her feet, standing guard in front of Toby. Hell would freeze over before she would allow anything to happen to him.

Where was that bastard Symes?

Toby blinked. The image of Jules standing in front of him with her weapon drawn and aimed shot a jolt of adrenaline through his system. The stress hormone gave him enough oomph to sit up, but he didn't want to surprise Jules, so he coughed and then asked, "What is it? What's happening?"

"Not sure yet," Jules responded. The tension in her voice said she was strung tight and ready to snap. "It's a dot moving toward us."

He squinted in the direction her weapon pointed as he drew his own Glock. For a split second, he forgot about the wrist injury in addition to the potentially broken arm. The swelling was worse. The injury might hold him back, but he could still aim and shoot with his left hand. Getting his Glock out of the holster caused brain-splitting, headache-inducing pain like he'd never experienced.

"You're making yourself too big of a target," he pointed out. "You need to get lower."

"I will when this person gets close enough to shoot at us," she said. "I squat down right now, and he disappears from my view."

"How do you know he'll shoot?" he asked.

"Symes got my backup weapon." The admission was followed by a sharp sigh.

"Could have been a lot worse," he pointed out. Every law enforcement agent or officer had the nightmare of being shot with their own weapon at one time or another during their careers. Jules had explained hers in detail after a beer at dinner one night. Wouldn't happen as long as he had air in his lungs. "I don't see anything."

"Exactly," she said.

Right. He was too low.

"Are you sure the dot is human?" he asked.

"No idea," she admitted. "But I'm not willing to take any chances."

Fair point. Jules was one of the best marshals he'd ever worked with. She didn't think so, but then, she was too hard on herself. "Could be debris blowing around down there."

"Are you willing to take that chance?" she asked.

"If my legs worked like they're supposed to, I'd circle around and try to catch the bastard unaware from behind," he said. It would take some of the burden off Jules while ensuring the perp was back in custody.

"Stay put," she suggested. "You'll do more good here than trying to run off half-cocked while you're hurt."

Those words couldn't be denied. He'd end up a liability, possibly putting Jules in more danger. Frustration nailed him at not being more help. He grabbed hold of a door handle on the chopper and pulled up to standing. He leaned his back against the metal. It wouldn't be long before critters and vultures came for Captain Crawford. The thought of being picked apart by scavengers sent a mental image Toby wouldn't soon forget. It was a fate the good pilot didn't deserve.

Jules swore. "Whatever it is decided to change direction."

The spot hung a right. Was he trying to come up behind them? The land on the other side of the chopper was relatively flat. "This area doesn't get a whole lot of rain."

"How do you know that? What are you, *Farmer's Almanac*?" Jules quipped.

"My dad took me and Lila camping here a few times when we were kids," he stated. "Weird facts like that stick in my head."

"I didn't know you guys camped as kids, let alone came here," she said, diligently watching the dot that was becoming smaller by the second. All she knew about Lila was that she'd died five years ago. Toby didn't talk about his sister.

"Can't tell you everything about my past," he said with a laugh—a laugh that hurt like hell. His ribs ached, no doubt having taken a blow during the crash when he landed on the ground. A flash of the chopper spinning out of control stamped his brain.

There was a lot that he kept to himself about his past despite telling Jules almost everything else about him. He'd been tempted. It was a little too easy to talk to her. They'd closed down a bar one night, and he'd damn near told her everything. He'd stopped himself when he realized he couldn't stand her looking at him like the failure he was after letting his sister down.

Not Jules.

She still looked at him like he was a good human being, a protector. Someone who was capable of doing anything he set his mind to.

Hell, a hero.

Shame shrouded him like the dark, heavy clouds wrapped the hilltop in the distance. That night in the bar, he'd stopped himself in time. It was the reason he didn't casually go out for a beer with her anymore.

He'd gotten a little too comfortable with Jules.

"Whatever it was, it's gone now," Jules said, breaking into his heavy thoughts. She holstered her weapon and turned to face him. "Now, we need to take care of your injuries before you lose consciousness on me again."

He opened his mouth to argue, but she stopped him with a hand in the air. Their gazes locked. For a split second, he felt a familiar jolt. The electricity and warmth that followed touched the depths of him.

It was the reason he joked with her instead of taking a serious tone. He had to keep their interactions lighthearted.

Fortunately for him, they didn't work together often.

It made life easier when she didn't stand so close that he could reach out and touch her. Or smell her unique scent— a mix of citrus and jasmine—when the wind blew in his direction.

Toby cleared his throat to ease some of the dryness. "I feel like I ate a pound of dirt."

"I've been collecting water," Jules said. "We should probably drink some so I can collect more. If what you said is true about the rain, it could stop any minute, and we won't get a refill anytime soon."

Toby tilted his head back and opened his mouth to catch a few raindrops as Jules retrieved a thermal mug.

"Here, take as much as you need," she said to him.

"When was the last time you drank water?" he asked, figuring, as always, Jules was taking care of someone else instead of herself.

"I was waiting for it to fill up more," she said before catching his gaze. "Since we might be here for a while, do you mind telling me why criminals like Symes get to you so much?"

It was just like Jules to cut to the chase when she was curious about a topic. This subject had been off-limits to her and everyone else.

Could he open those old wounds?

Chapter Three

Rain battered down. Winds kicked up. Without communication to the outside world, Jules had no idea how long the storm would last. Or when help would arrive, if ever.

"Let's hop inside the back of the chopper and get out of this storm system," Toby said, instead of answering her question outright. Changing the subject was classic Toby.

Jules hesitated before climbing inside. For one, there was a dead man inside. As much as she didn't want to leave Captain Crawford alone until help arrived, being in close proximity to someone once they'd passed sent creepy-crawlies up her spine. But staying outside in the elements left them vulnerable. With winds whipping around, debris could slam into one of them or both. They might not see it coming until the last minute, making it nearly impossible to get out of the way. Then there was the age-old wisdom advising against standing next to a window in a severe thunderstorm. The chopper had windows—pressurized, thank goodness—and the small cabin would ensure she sat next to one.

Was it safe?

"Visibility is next to nothing," she pointed out as she climbed inside and settled in the back on the floorboard. She faced the back so she wouldn't have to look at Captain

Crawford. "We won't know if Symes is coming back until he's right up on us now."

Jules extended a hand to help Toby up. He took it and, with serious effort, made it inside and out of the pounding rain. The chopper offered a temporary shelter at best, and she noticed he was nursing his right arm.

Did she dare pin all her hopes on being rescued?

"We should sit back-to-back," Toby offered.

Jules complied. "Keep your arm above your heart to help with swelling."

The reality of his wrist being broken and not just angry meant the swelling wasn't likely to go down.

No phone to call for medical help. No way to reach her supervisor. No way to contact her family. *Family.* The fact her grandparents were lying in hospital beds fighting for their lives while she was out here hit full force. She had to push those unproductive thoughts aside.

The knot tightened in her chest. Would Symes circle back to the only known shelter in the area like a scavenger waiting for its prey to die so it could pick at the carcass without risking injury? Were they sitting ducks?

Toby grunted.

"We need to take a look at that broken arm," Jules reminded him. "There must be an emergency kit in here somewhere."

"Small, private aircraft aren't required by law to keep supplies," Toby pointed out. "I've been on some that didn't carry a Band-Aid. And turns out, it's my wrist, not my arm. Not as bad as I initially thought."

"It's broken, Toby. Let's hope Captain Crawford erred on the safety side of the equation."

Jules climbed around on all fours toward the very back. She felt around in the darkness. Then she remembered Toby's phone. There might not be bars, but it could still come in handy. "Toss me your cell."

He did.

She caught it and flicked on the flashlight app.

The battery was low, 29 percent. They would need to conserve until an emergency crew could locate them.

She spotted a white case with the telltale red cross on it. "Found it."

The ten-inch-by-twelve-inch box had aspirin, ibuprofen and an assortment of Band-Aids. The real score was the self-adhesive wrap. She could create a basic sling with it for Toby's arm, which might help keep him from using it.

"Take your jacket off," Jules said to Toby.

He smirked. "Whatever you say, gorgeous."

Jules cracked a smile despite herself. The man always knew how to make her laugh and lighten the darkest circumstances. Except when rapists were mentioned. He never joked when the subject came up, and he still wouldn't talk about why.

With a grunt, he managed to shrug out of his blazer. In a jacket and jeans, he was devastatingly handsome. Jules had no idea why the man wasn't out every weekend with a new person. The women at the office lined up to speak to him. Every time he entered the room, their fingers curled into their hair, voices raised several pitches higher and smiles widened in a show of teeth named, rightfully so, The Teeth Show.

And yet he preferred to stay home on Friday nights and hang out with friends most weekends. When he did go on a date, he never discussed the details with her. So, she kept her dating life secret as well. *Dating life?* That was a generous term for the occasional dinner out when she forced herself to swipe on a dating app and received a match.

Since her career took up most of her time and she preferred silence to sitting across the table from a stranger forcing conversation over a meal, she did very little swiping. Plus, she'd rather spend Saturday night watching a movie with friends, if she felt like going out at all.

"I can't sit here and do nothing," Toby said while she worked on his wrist.

She didn't stop, didn't respond.

Toby brought his good hand up and closed his fingers around the small of her wrist. Her gaze met his—bad idea this close—and he used those used-to-getting-what-he-wanted eyes on her.

"Hey, no, it's not going to work," Jules protested. "We don't know which way he went, and we have no cell service out here. Not to mention your phone has very little battery left. Twenty-nine percent, Toby."

It was classic Toby for his phone to be near dead. He'd borrowed hers enough times when his died. She should have known.

Toby didn't budge.

"We'll never find him out here," she continued, realizing she'd already lost the battle. "Fine, then. How do you expect to locate Symes?"

"Easy," Toby remarked. "All we have to do is wait out the rain. It'll be cold and he'll be wet, so he'll figure out how to start a fire."

"He has no supplies," she pointed out. "And everything is wet. How the hell do you expect him to start a fire?"

"This man has evaded capture for eleven years, Jules. He will figure out how to stay alive under all conditions."

True enough, Symes was believed to have spent time in the mountains in Colorado during winter with no known shelter, as well as Montana. This guy had a few tricks up his sleeve. He was smart. He knew how to thrive under harsh conditions.

Facing a lifetime sentence if recaptured, he had nothing to lose. The combination was dangerous, and the reason US marshals were shot at more than any other agency.

Toby winced as she wrapped his hand and arm against his body to keep them secure and from moving. "He might have been in this area before multiple times. He could know the lay of the land. Eleven years of hiding with every agency hunting him is no small accomplishment."

Toby made more good points there.

"Okay, fine," she conceded. "We go after him once the storm lets up."

They couldn't exactly stay inside the chopper forever. The harsh truth was help might not be on its way. They might be stuck here for days before anyone actually located them in the vastness of this national park, if at all.

Symes could realistically come after them.

She sat back on her heels, assessing her work. "Try not to move it, okay?"

"I'll do my best," he responded.

"Rest is probably out of the question." She figured Symes could be working his way back to them right now.

Toby wiggled his eyebrows at her, trying to pull a laugh out of her.

When it didn't work, he turned on those serious honeybrowns. "You know we can't sit around and wait for him to come for us. There will be clues as to which direction he went. My guess is that he didn't go very far. He'll circle back at some point just to see if we're alive, unless…"

It was almost as though Toby couldn't say the words.

"Unless he finds a family or a couple, kills them, and then steals their vehicle," she said after a sharp exhalation.

Toby was right about one thing. They couldn't let Symes roam around by himself. He was a danger to others, and she couldn't stand idly by while he took another life or lives.

They were going to have to go out there and find him.

"ARM'S GOOD AND the rain has slowed." Toby couldn't stand sitting around while Symes was free. "We should get going after we clean and bandage your injury."

"Hold on there a minute, sir." Jules's serious voice wasn't something to mess around with. Toby had learned the hard way. "I have medicine that will help with the pain, so don't give me the your-body-is-a-temple speech, because we're not attending to me or leaving unless you take an ibuprofen. Deal?"

Toby knew when he'd lost an argument before it started. He held out his hand, palm up.

Jules was a miracle worker. She produced two pills and more water before dropping her gaze. "What do we do with him?" She motioned toward Captain Crawford.

"I'm sorry, Jules. There's nothing that can be done with the supplies we have right now." It was awful. Toby didn't want to abandon the pilot either. There was no way to revive him. Sticking around to hold vigil while a rapist-murderer was on the loose wouldn't bring the man back. A tough decision had to be made to save the living, no matter how awful a position that was to be in.

Toby hung his head. "It's the worst."

"Should we move him?" she asked. "He looks uncomfortable."

"It's not a good idea," he said.

"What about leaving something behind so people know to look for us if someone happens across the site?" she asked.

"First of all, we need to take a look at the gash on your forehead," he said, turning the tables. "You get to be the patient now."

The slight pout to full lips said she wasn't thrilled about being on the other side of the proverbial stethoscope.

"You're going to have to help me out," he said. "Can you open the antiseptic wipes?"

Jules picked up the packet and then ripped it open before handing over the contents. He managed to separate the two sheets of cleaner, using one to clean his hands and the other to wipe away dirt and grime on and around the cut.

A sense of urgency was building to finish up and get out there. Symes could be miles away by now, or he might have collapsed just outside of view.

Either way, Toby wanted the bastard back in handcuffs. He'd physically sit on top of Symes until help arrived, if he had to.

Once the rain cleared, Toby would also watch for buzzards. They would signal if Symes was out there dead.

"Antibiotic ointment next," he said after picking through the supplies. "Open, please."

Jules did without argument. He suspected she was just as eager to figure out what had happened to Symes as he was. Jules had always been more cautious, though. She did a better job of balancing out risk.

After opening the small tube of ointment, she dabbed some of it on his finger, then winced as he touched her forehead. He couldn't risk infection, especially if they had to survive out here for a few days.

Leaving the relative safety of the chopper was a calculated risk. Soon enough, Crawford's body would begin to deteriorate and attract critters starved for a meal. Out here, it would be survival of the fittest. The promise of fresh meat would tempt predators within range.

The thought gave Toby the willies. Once he was gone from this earth, he didn't want to know what happened to his body. With the risk in his job, he always assumed he'd go out on duty. Some felon along the way would end up using him for target practice so they could escape and would nail him with a lucky shot.

Despite safety protocol, there were inherent risks associated with this job. Risks that he took seriously but also didn't want to focus on too hard. He'd learned a long time ago the secret to living as long as he had was to keep making plans for the future. His included a cold beer, his couch and a football game.

"All right," he said. "Grab supplies and put them in your backpack. We can leave the first aid kit open with stuff we don't need so people know someone rummaged through it."

Jules took in a deep breath, like she always did before she jumped into something that scared her.

"I'm right here," he reassured her. "I'll be alongside you the whole way. We'll find the son of a bitch."

"Did something happen to you when you were younger?" she asked as they exited the chopper.

Standing up made his head spin. "Not me personally. No. But someone I was responsible for."

"That's the reason, isn't it?"

She deserved to know that he wouldn't stop until either Symes was back in custody or Toby was dead.

"Yes," he said, staring out as the rain dissipated. Visibility was still low.

"Was he caught?" she asked.

It might be the circumstances or the fact he might never get another chance to tell Jules or anyone else what had happened that suddenly had him wanting to get it off his chest. He paused to get a grip on the anger that always flooded him when he thought about what had happened.

"What did I tell you about how my sister died?" he asked, avoiding answering her question.

"Accident," she said as they started down the hill. Going this way made the most sense because the opposite side was too flat. It would be too easy to be seen for long distances. Symes would take the hilly route with lots of large rocks to hide behind in case bullets started flying. He'd head toward the mountains.

"I lied," he admitted.

"Why?" The hurt in her voice cut to the quick.

"Because I don't tell anyone what really happened," he countered, but it was a weak excuse to give his best friend.

"Didn't realize I was *anyone* to you, Toby."

"Lila was raped by someone who taunted me for becoming a US marshal," he continued, hoping she could understand once she heard the whole truth.

"Oh, no," Jules said, her tone so soft it wrapped around him, comforting him. "I'm so sorry."

He didn't deserve it.

"Be sorry for Lila," he countered, armor up. "Not me."

"I'm sorry for both of you," Jules said with more of that warmth in her tone.

"I'm the reason she's dead." Moisture gathered in his eyes, which he quickly sniffed away. He coughed to cover the frog in his throat.

"That's impossible."

"I told her to fight back if she ever found herself being compromised," he managed to get out. The memory crashed around him, shattering him. "She wasn't the type to stand up for herself. Lila was always putting everyone else above herself. If anything ever happened, I was afraid she'd freeze up, so I told her to fight like hell. She had to have been so damn scared." He stopped for a few seconds to collect his thoughts and stop the emotions threatening to bombard him. "But she put up a valiant fight."

"That was good advice, Toby."

"Once the bastard raped her, he murdered her." His voice cracked. *Pull it together, man.* "It should have been me."

"Did they catch the son of a bitch?" Jules asked in measured calmness.

"Lila managed to scratch his face up," he said, shaking his head. "She lived long enough to identify a tattoo on the perp's neck of the outline of a dark-haired woman's face and neck embracing the head and torso of a skeleton just below her. The FBI decided it was a sick reference to his many faceless victims embracing their deaths." He'd checked the necks of every single rapist he'd ever gone after.

Jules got quiet. Too quiet.

"What is it? What's going on?"

"How certain are you about those details?" she asked.

"She could barely speak," he said. "It was the best the cop on the scene could make out."

"What if the tattoo wasn't on his neck but was on his forearm?" she asked. "And it wasn't a skeleton but was the grim reaper instead?"

Toby had a bad feeling about where this might be going. "Why do you ask?"

"Symes."

Chapter Four

Could Symes have been the one to rape and murder Toby's sister? Icy fingers gripped Jules at the thought of the perp they'd been transporting being the one to cause such heartache and pain to Toby and his family.

"Does that moth—"

"It might not be the same person," Jules countered. "We can't be certain of anything right now."

Toby ground his back teeth so hard she heard them over the driving rain. He sat there, silent, for a long moment.

"Tell me more about what happened," Jules gently urged.

"Why?" Toby bit out. His tone was the equivalent of sharp knives stabbing her in the chest. Toby was the only person on the planet who could affect her in that way. He could turn on the charm one minute and light her on fire in the next without flexing a muscle. Then there was the side that could hurt her with words as sharp as daggers.

Did he realize the effect he had on her?

Jules decided he didn't because Toby wasn't the kind of person who would treat her emotions like a kid's toy. She'd never felt so vulnerable with any other human being, so there was definitely something special about the man, because no one else got under her skin. For the first two years of their friendship, she'd chalked it up to being best friends and caring too much about what he thought of her. Last year, she'd realized there was more to it but refused to fully admit how deep her feelings ran even to herself. Because what good would it do to go there when it wouldn't be reciprocated?

Besides, Toby always kept part of himself closed off to everyone, out of bounds. In three years, she'd never been able to break through. Despite sharing what he had just now, he'd already closed up.

"Because we're friends, Toby," she said out of frustration. "Isn't that a good enough reason?"

"It won't bring her back," he countered, holding on to every bit of hurt and anger as though time couldn't heal every wound.

"No," she agreed, softening her tone as she realized just how much pain he was in and how much he blamed himself for something outside of his control. *But it might just bring* you *back.* That part of Toby that he kept to himself also kept the rest of the world at arm's length. Their friendship could only go so deep before the wall came up between them again.

Not that Jules was much better.

"Talk to me, Toby," she pressed, glancing back at the captain. Life was short. Careers like theirs could cut the timeline in half. Symes could be sneaking up on them right now, and they wouldn't be the wiser. "We're here, together, and it might just be our—"

"We'll get out of this mess alive," Toby said, cutting her off, not accepting any other possibility.

"I know," she said, half-heartedly. It was probably her grandparents' situation that had her realizing how quickly life could change or be lost. In a snap, the people she loved most could be gone forever.

"They'll be okay too," Toby said as though reading her thoughts. It was a good thing he couldn't read all of them, or she would be busted. Her attraction was something she kept at bay, but then, women who were attracted to Toby formed a long line. He had to know she thought he was sex on a stick, even though his ego remained remarkably in check.

"What if they don't pull through?" she asked, going with the shift in conversation as they waited out the storm.

"We'll deal with it as a team," he reassured her. "Just like the way you helped me when I lost my grandmother." He'd been raised by grandparents too, which was one of many things they had in common. His grandmother had been his last living relative.

The way he put it made it sound like she was less alone, but she *was* alone. At the end of the day, she went home to an empty town house. Toby did the same, but he liked it that way. Said he could think better when he was by himself. There were times when she wondered how true his statement was, despite his commitment to the words as he spoke them. He overcommitted as if he was trying to convince himself the line was true.

Jules got it. She hyped herself up for a workout at the gym using the same tactic. *Speak it if you want to believe it* was the philosophy.

A crack of lightning caused her to tense, bringing her current reality front and center in her thoughts.

Toby was severely injured. As much as he wanted to go after Symes, how long could Toby last? How far would he be able to go in his current condition?

He was iron-man tough, but everyone had limits. Injuries could only be set aside for so long. Adrenaline had a limited life. And then what?

They could end up lost with no shelter, food or water.

On the flip side, they might find a family or individual camping before Symes did. They could potentially receive assistance, medical care and a way to communicate with the outside world. Stay here and Symes could retrace his steps to them. Because another possibility was that he might be just as injured as the two of them. He might not have found anything useful out there. He could have no other choice but to return. Killing them may not have been on his agenda at first, but much like Texas weather, that could change.

Examining all sides of a situation helped with important decisions.

"How long do you think it's safe to sit here?" she asked, also realizing they were the equivalent of sitting ducks in this downpour.

"Before we move on, you can talk to me about your grandparents anytime, Jules," Toby said with the kind of compassion that tightened the knot in her stomach. She didn't want to need him. "You know that, right?"

"Nothing to discuss," Jules stated, realizing she'd just pulled the same trick of shutting down that was classic Toby. Was it another reason they got along so well? They were kindred spirits?

It was also another strong reason they should never date. Losing Toby—most relationships ended, especially when it came to Jules's love life—would destroy her. Keeping him in the friend zone was the only way to go the distance. Because she couldn't imagine her life without him in it.

"I know," he said with a wince as he moved to turn toward her.

"Give me the truth, Toby," she started. "On a scale of one to ten, how's the pain?"

"A three," he said with a smile that was so good at disarming her. Ever since the revelation about Symes possibly being the one who'd killed Lila, there was an unfamiliar tone to his voice, even when he attempted to be light-hearted. At least he was talking now. Silence was much worse.

"This isn't golf," she countered.

"Okay, seriously," he said. "On a scale of one to ten, I'm looking at about a twenty." He quickly added, "But we both know I've dealt with worse."

"Than a chopper crash?" she shot back. "I doubt it."

The rain lashed against the glass. Winds kicked up. A loud thud sent her pulse racing and her adrenaline soaring.

Locking gazes with Toby was always a mistake this close, but Jules did it anyway.

"Stay here," he said. "I'll go check it out."

"Over my dead body you're going alone." Those words had a haunting ring to them, Jules realized a little too late. She could only pray they weren't foreshadowing what was to come.

Toby shoved aside a moment of doubt as he palmed his weapon in his left hand. Since his right one was temporarily trashed, he'd have to make do with his less dominant side. They were tall on risk and short on options, not to mention the fact Symes might be getting away.

"Let's do this," he said to Jules before rolling over and kicking the door open. At least both of his legs worked. That was a plus.

As he watched Jules climb out of the chopper, he noticed she favored her left leg.

"Everything all right?" he asked, motioning toward the knee.

She pulled up her slacks to reveal a swollen knee. "Damn. It's the size of a melon. How did I miss that?" She took a couple of tentative steps, wincing as she attempted to put pressure on her left side. "That's not good." A moment of panic crossed her features before she regained composure and then grabbed a couple of pills from the emergency kit. "Looks like you're not the only one in need of ibuprofen."

"Hand me your backpack," he said to her after she swallowed the medicine.

Jules placed the emergency kit inside before handing the bag over. Toby shouldered the pack on his left side without setting down his weapon, which was a miracle. Maneuvering around hurt like hell, but he was mobile. He'd survive. Once they located Symes—because Toby had no plans to stop searching until the bastard was back in cuffs—he could think about getting proper medical attention.

From the corner of his eye, he noticed a piece of metal. He walked over to check it out. "This is where Symes dumped his handcuffs."

Jules joined him. "Dammit." With effort, she bent down and felt around on the ground. Came up with a key. "Looks like he managed to strip my ankle gun and the key." She shivered. "Thinking about the creep's hands on me at all gives me the willies."

It sent white-hot fire licking through Toby's veins. Losing his sister to a rapist had messed with his head for years and would for the rest of his life. He couldn't fathom Jules in a similar fate. Grinding his back teeth to the point they might crack, Toby managed to say, "Let's go find this human piece of garbage. It's time to take out the trash."

"Agreed."

"Symes might not be far, so keep on the lookout," Toby warned. The man had to have sustained some injuries during the crash, which might have slowed him down. Clearly, it didn't stop him, though.

The rain continued to batter them, hurling big splotches down on the earth. Despite the ibuprofen, movement shot pain rocketing through Toby's body.

Nothing would stop him from hunting down Symes.

"It's anyone's guess which way he took off," Jules said. "We might as well head this way." She motioned down the hill to a ravine.

"Good idea," he confirmed. "It's easier to head downhill than up or across since the terrain in this area is rocky."

"Visibility is low," she pointed out. "We'll want to keep close to each other."

The easiest way to attack them at this point would be to divide and conquer, so Jules was thinking down the right path. "Will do."

Since walking—or any movement, for that matter—wasn't going to get any easier, Toby sucked in a breath and headed down. The path was crooked and rocky, so Symes could be waiting behind a boulder to strike. Even with a weapon at the ready, Toby was at a disadvantage with his right arm being held against his body. It made keeping balance a challenge. Shooting left-handed was going to be interesting if the need arose.

Toby would cross that bridge when he came to it. For now, it was all he could do not to bite it as he navigated the rocky hill.

Water would be somewhere below, which wasn't a concern given the current weather conditions. Hikers and families would make a campsite near a stream. The thought of an unsuspecting family being tortured or killed got Toby's legs moving faster.

Symes was a twisted bastard. The thought Toby might be close to catching the man who'd haunted his nightmares for years sent more adrenaline thumping through him, giving him a much-needed boost.

Jules wasn't far behind. He wanted—no, needed—to keep her close. The easy explanation was that he was concerned for another law enforcement officer's safety. That was the easy way out. Jules had been a lifeline during his grandmother's Alzheimer's diagnosis. Jules had stayed by his side while he had to make decisions no grandson wanted to have to make on his beloved family member's behalf. And Jules had been the only reason he'd made it through the storm of emotions that flooded him as he watched his grandmother's casket be lowered into the ground.

So, it was far more than friendship between them. Jules was the closest thing to family he had left in this world. She meant the world to him.

Toby's foot slipped. Instinct had him trying to use his dominant hand, which landed him hard on his backside.

Sliding, he leaned back and went with the flow. It was all he could do without ditching his gun. So, he didn't fight against the fall.

By the time he stopped, Jules was so far up the hill that he could no longer hear her. Lightning streaked across the gray sky, but the flash gave him a visual on Jules. She was coming down as fast as her legs could go as pebbles came down in a landslide.

"Are you okay?" she shouted. Making noise was a mistake, despite the ceiling of rain and the insulation it provided. Otherwise, her voice would have carried for miles in this area. He should know. Lila had tested the waters by standing on the largest boulder she could find and shouting at the top of her lungs. She'd been ten years old the last time they camped here with their father.

First, Toby had lost his mother. Then he'd lost his father. His sister was the third to go but the most difficult to take. His mother had succumbed to recurring breast cancer. His father had died of a broken heart, according to Toby's grandmother, but that had taken another five years and a back injury that ended with his father being addicted to painkillers. Alcohol and pain medication were the worst kind of bedfellows. His sister had died a tragic death, leaving the once family of four down to a lone person standing.

Then he lost his grandmother too. Alzheimer's claimed her memories, which was a whole different type of slow, drawn-out death, despite only lasting a year after the official diagnosis. Her memory had been slipping long before that, and she'd become confused.

Jules had stayed in the spare bedroom at his grandmother's house during the last couple of months. And now he wanted to return the favor by helping her with her grandparents' situation if she'd let him.

A pebble slammed against the crown of his head, causing him to quickly sit up. Pain reminded him that he was alive, so he normally took it in stride. But the pebble felt like it had cracked his skull.

As Jules neared, her gaze focused on a spot below his. Determination replaced panic.

"What do you see?" he asked. Had they just found their felon?

Chapter Five

Something moved. Jules couldn't see clearly enough to determine if it was animal or human. But something had shifted position, moving behind a boulder and out of view.

A tingle raced up her spine. It was the kind of sensation that sparked every time she got close to her mark. A shot of adrenaline caused her senses to heighten, becoming razor-sharp. Her head stopped hurting, and she no longer felt the pain in her swollen knee. Good signs? Probably not.

In fact, she knew they weren't, but the temporary relief was welcome anyway. A brief reprieve was better than none.

Hunkering down to make herself as small a target as possible, she slipped next to a boulder in case the person or thing below was Symes. Any manner of wild animal could be out here. Between black bears, bobcats and mountain lions, there were plenty of predators that could take advantage of her weakened condition. The great equalizer was her service weapon. Toby could defend himself as well.

Was it a mistake to leave the chopper, where they could barricade themselves inside? It would have provided enough shelter to keep them safe from wildlife.

Considering most of Big Bend was a desert, the rain

coming down was unusual for this climate. Did that mean it would stop soon?

Almost the second she had the thought, Mother Nature complied. At least they were getting a break there. The sky was still dark and moody, but visibility increased enough to see something behind the boulder. Hiding? Waiting? Biding its time?

Jules moved past Toby, who sat very still. They made brief eye contact. Enough to communicate she needed to move very slowly and carefully, and he had her back. If she had to be lost in a desert with anyone, she would want it to be Toby. Words weren't necessary in a tense situation with him, unlike with other marshals she'd worked with, where ground rules had to be set early on before anything went down. She and Toby could anticipate each other's moves with one look. Being in sync had never been a problem.

A rock caused Jules to slip. Her bad knee buckled. She caught herself in time to avoid biting it, but pebbles tumbled down the narrow path. Whatever waited would know someone was coming now.

Sucking in a breath, Jules righted herself and then pressed her back against the boulder. Methodically, she made her way down to the spot where someone or something had been a few moments before.

Whatever had been there was gone now.

Frustration bit at her as Toby joined her. She shook her head. He frowned, clamping his mouth shut. Without a word, he took the lead and kept moving forward. As the adrenaline boost wore off, Jules felt every bit of the pain in her knee. Her head pounded like a two-year-old with a new drum set. Those ibuprofen pills weren't nearly enough to tackle this pain. If they could keep some of the inflammation down in her knee, she'd be happy.

Half an hour later, they'd made it down to a ravine.

Toby sat down on a nearby rock. He set down his weapon and retrieved a bottle of water out of the backpack, offering it to her first.

Jules took the bottle, twisted off the cap and held it above her lips as she drank the cool liquid. Her clothes stuck to her like a wet swimsuit. Clumps of hair clung to her face. She was a drowned rat at this point.

After handing the bottle back to Toby, she scanned the area once more. The rain washed away any tracks the culprit might have otherwise left, leaving the question of animal or human unanswered.

"This area only gets about ten inches of rain per year," Toby pointed out. "Didn't realize all ten inches came at the same time."

"I think the weatherperson can tick that box," she quipped before cracking a small smile. A break in tension was much needed. There was no one better at cracking through the most serious situations and infusing humor. It was a survival mechanism that worked to bring down heightened emotions so you could think clearly again. Putting yourself in a calmer state helped you return to problem-solving mode, which spawned the best ideas.

"You sure about that?" he asked with one of those devastating smiles that was all Toby. It might not reach his eyes, but that didn't lessen the impact. Toby smiles had a way of releasing dozens of butterflies in her chest while her stomach simultaneously performed a national-champion-level gymnastics routine.

Jules took a hard look at the sky. "I don't know, man.

Maybe we need a little more." She stuck her tongue out. "I'd like to catch a few more drops, if you know what I mean."

Catching Symes had been the find of the year—hell, the decade. Which made losing him all that much harder to swallow. People would say it wasn't their fault. But he'd been in their custody. People would say the chopper crash was an accident. But it had been their responsibility to bring him in. People would say she should give herself a break. But she wouldn't sleep at night until this bastard was caught. If he managed to escape and live, he would pick right back up where he'd left off, raping and killing innocent women. Their blood would be on Jules's hands. How was she supposed to let herself off the hook for that?

"We'll catch him," Toby reassured her.

"How did you know what I was thinking?" she asked, surprised at how easy it seemed to be for him to figure out what was on her mind. Toby clued in to everything but her attraction.

"You get a tiny wrinkle on your forehead when you're deep in thought and being hard on yourself," he explained. "And small brackets around your mouth."

"I do?"

"Yes," he confirmed. "It's not hard to figure out the topic considering our circumstances, the fact we think alike when it comes to work, and the reality that I'm over here beating myself up for the same reason."

He got away.

"All good points," she said, realizing she did know he would be thinking along the same lines.

"The captain's death isn't your fault either," he added.

"What makes you think I blame myself?" she asked.

"Because I'm doing the same thing." He looked up to the sky. "I have no idea what happens to us when we…"

He let his sentence hang in the air.

"But I sure hope my family is back together, laughing," he said in a rare emotional moment. "I hope they're at peace."

"What about you, Toby?" she asked.

"Some people don't deserve to be let off the hook," he said, his voice almost a whisper.

"I've messed up plenty in my life and line of work," she said, not ready to accept his answer. For the first time—and maybe it was the circumstances—she wanted to push for a better response. "Do I deserve to be forgiven?"

"Of course you do," he said, like it was common knowledge.

"You sure about that?" she pressed.

"One hundred percent," he said as the arch in his brow shot up sky-high. "Why would you even question it?"

"Because I can't forgive myself for not being bedside for my grandparents right now," she said.

"You will be once we locate Symes," he pointed out. A flash of hatred crossed behind his eyes at the mention of the man's name. "Not being there isn't your fault. The accident certainly wasn't your fault. You and your siblings have worked out a plan to have coverage 24/7. You get updates on your cell as well as phone calls." He issued a thoughtful pause. "Plus, there's nothing you can do at the hospital except sit and worry. Focusing on your job keeps your mind occupied until they wake up."

"Keep talking like that and I'll think you've given this situation a lot of thought," she teased. Though, his reassurances meant the world to her.

"I think about every situation that involves you," he said with a hint of vulnerability in his voice. Before Jules could respond, he added, "You're my best friend, kiddo."

Leave it to Toby to make certain she didn't confuse friendship with anything more. He'd always been clear about his intentions and how he felt about her.

Friendship was good, though. It would last. And she needed him more than ever while facing the situation with her grandparents.

"Speaking of Symes," she said, clearing her throat. "What's our next move?" She added the word *buddy* in her mind as a reminder. It was good to keep herself in check when it came to how she viewed Toby, because it was all too easy to cross a line and convince herself that he wanted more.

Toby leaned against the boulder, forcing his thoughts away from the pain in his wrist. *Doesn't hurt. I'm good. I'm good. I'm good.* Repeating the mantra had gotten him past a few tough sports injuries in his youth. Could it work now?

At this point, he'd try anything to ease the pain that a couple of ibuprofens couldn't make a dent in.

The image of Lila forced its way front and center. First, her innocent smile. She'd been protected all her life. Toby had deemed himself her guardian after their father sank into a dark hole following his wife's death.

Lila had been dubbed their miracle child since Toby's mother had had a hard pregnancy with him and wasn't supposed to be able to have more children. Apparently, she'd been warned it would be too dangerous for her body to go through it a second time. And that was the rub. His mother had survived pregnancy and childbirth only to be taken by breast cancer before her miracle child entered kindergarten.

A newly minted teenager by that point, Toby would have been rebellious as hell if his baby sister hadn't grounded him. Their grandmother was aging. Their father was gone, for all intents and purposes. Caring for Lila had fallen to Toby. The reality was that he didn't mind. She had given him purpose that was otherwise lacking in his turned-upside-down world.

It had been impossible to turn his back on those innocent brown eyes as she stood at the kitchen door waiting for their mother to return home from the hospital, completely unaware of what he already knew. Their beautiful, loving mother wasn't coming home.

Becoming Lila's caretaker had given him purpose, marching orders. Look what he'd done to return the favor.

"Hey," Jules said, cutting into his heavy thoughts—thoughts he'd been able to hold at bay in recent years. The possibility—however remote it might be—that Symes was responsible for Lila's murder brought back all those haunting memories.

It was time justice was served. For Lila. Toby owed her that much.

"Where did you go just now?" Jules asked as Toby refocused, looking at her instead of the sky that seemed to go on forever.

He didn't respond. What could he say? That if they found Symes, he couldn't be certain he wouldn't mete out his own form of justice, born from a need that had been simmering for more years than he cared to count.

Jules studied him. "You all right?"

Normally, she was good at reading his emotions too. But this hatred ran deep. She didn't know this side of Toby. He'd kept his darkness away from her because Jules had been the only peek of light in his life. He wanted to hang on to it. Let her keep believing he was a great person who always did the right thing.

But when he came face-to-face with Symes again, Toby couldn't be held responsible for his actions. Not when the image of his little sister's life being choked out of her after being brutalized haunted him.

"I will be," Toby finally answered after a pause.

Chapter Six

Jules got the impression the sentence was left unfinished. She'd seen him go quiet before. It seemed like a good time to give him space. He'd go dark on her for a couple of hours—sometimes a day, if they were off work—and then he would resurface like nothing had happened. "Right now, though, we need to get on the move."

Jules decided not to keep prodding. He would talk when he was ready.

"Let's go find a water source," he said. "Water is the ultimate life-giving source, but it takes lives too. It only takes seconds to drown."

Jules took note of the change in Toby's tone and decided to ask him about it later.

Symes most likely beat them to the punch. He had a head start, which gave him an advantage. A lingering thought as to why he didn't kill them when he had the chance sat heavily in the back of her thoughts.

She would let it marinate. See if any plausible reason stood out other than the simple explanation that said he plainly thought they would die either way. Killing them was unnecessary when nature would take care of it. The easy answer was usually the right one, so she settled on that for now and ignored the niggling feeling there could be something else to it.

Heading farther down was a slow, methodical process.

How had Symes made the trek? A bigger question followed. Were they even on the right track?

Toby's reasoning made sense. Symes would want to find water. He must have left the crash site in a hurry, because he'd walked away from her backpack and medical supplies. A weapon would have been a priority. He'd managed to steal her SIG. Why not fire a few shots before taking off?

Because a wild animal scared him off.

Or had Jules stirred?

Jules had never seen an emptiness in Toby's stare like the one she'd just witnessed, like he'd been filled with a sudden darkness. Should she have told him Symes might be the person who'd killed his sister?

In hindsight, it might not have been the best idea. Especially since she couldn't be certain one way or the other without proof.

Every step caused her head to pound a little harder. Much more and the pain would be blinding. Had Symes counted on that?

"Where did you say the tattoo was, and what did it look like?" Toby asked when he finally stopped to take a drink of water and lean back on a rock.

"I think the first question we need to ask is how reliable the investigators on the scene of your sister's…" She couldn't bring herself to say the words out loud that would certainly gut Toby. "You know what I mean?"

"Yes," he confirmed.

"Thanks for not making me say the words."

He nodded his understanding.

"Symes has the outline of a dark-haired woman's face

and neck embracing the head and torso of the grim reaper on his forearm," she supplied.

"The Bureau decided it was a sick reference to his many faceless victims embracing their deaths." Toby hung his head. "I've checked the necks of every single rapist I've gone after ever since." He shook his head as he avoided her gaze. "Lila managed to scratch his face up too. Symes has scars, but I assumed they were from other victims."

"Which could still be true," she said. "The tattoos are similar, but there's no concrete proof they are the same person." She studied him for a long moment, realized a losing battle when she entered one. "Do you need to be pulled from this case?"

"No."

"You seem to be losing all sense of objectivity, Toby."

"I won't deny there's a lot of truth to that statement," he agreed. "You can turn me in, write me up or do whatever you need to do to cover your backside. But I'm not leaving." He made a dramatic show of waving his hands in the air. "And, in case you haven't noticed, we're stuck in this together, whether we want to be or not."

"What the hell, Toby?" She couldn't hold back her anger. "Is that what you think? All I'm interested in is covering my butt?"

He issued a sharp sigh.

"Because we go back, and before today, we went deep. If that's changed, you should have given me a heads-up. Because I'm in this with you up to my eyeballs, and I need to know what I'm getting into." She huffed out a breath. "And, in case you didn't know this, I'm trying to cover *your* butt, not mine. You could lose your job over something like this."

He didn't speak, just stared out in the distance as though his gaze could magically cut through the low clouds.

"Not to mention your life if you go after him half-cocked, not thinking straight and while you're seriously injured," she continued, trying to break through. It was like trying to punch a fist through a six-inch-thick steel wall. The subject of his sister was sensitive. Her heart went out to Toby for his loss. The tragic manner in which his sister had died was unforgivable. But he couldn't take it out on someone who may or may not be responsible. It was their job to deliver the perp in one piece so he could stand trial. Everyone deserved a fair trial, even Symes, as much as she hated the fact. Was the justice system perfect? No. Of course not. But it was all they had at the moment. Usually, it worked.

"You don't have to worry about me." Toby's words came out like he was talking to someone he couldn't stand to be in the same room with, which made her realize he was in serious trouble. This case could take him down if he wasn't careful. And then what?

Toby would have nothing left. Not to mention the fact he wasn't the kind of person who abused his position.

"You're my best friend, Toby. Don't let this guy get inside your head," she pleaded.

"He's not," Toby replied, but the reassuring words were hollow. "I wouldn't let a scumbag like Symes force me to do anything I didn't want to, Jules. You should know me better than that by now. But I won't back down from him either. I'll do whatever it takes to ensure the bastard is punished for what he did to all his victims, as well as my sister, if it turns out he's the one."

There was so much anger and hurt in his demeanor, his words and his expression that Jules barely recognized him.

She tried to put herself in his position. What if this sick son of a bitch had killed her cousins Crystal or Abilene? Would she be able to objectively do her job?

The answer came instantly. No. Absolutely not. Especially if she'd seen images from the crime scene. They would burn into her skull, and she would see nothing but fire if she was in the same room with the man who'd snuffed out their lives after torturing them.

Being out here, there wasn't a whole helluva lot she could do about having Toby replaced. Normally, she would make the call on his behalf, because she wouldn't have the presence of mind to be able to pull herself off the case either. She, of all people, knew how Toby thought. They were similar in that way.

"I wouldn't be objective," she admitted, hoping Toby could be honest with himself as well.

"That's your problem," he replied in a tone that said the conversation was over. This wasn't the time to put up an argument or try to get him to see reason. All she could do was nod. When and if the time came, she would work hard to ensure Toby didn't do anything that could come back on him later. She would have to step up her game in order to protect her friend.

Blinded by his anger, he couldn't see the potential damage he could do to his career, let alone the rest of his life, if he didn't handle the situation properly.

Jules resolved not to allow any harm to come to Toby or his reputation. She couldn't lose him too.

TOBY DIDN'T NEED PITY, and he didn't need a guardian. He needed revenge for Lila. The urge to find Symes took over. He had to be here somewhere. The man had to be injured. Life couldn't be so cruel as to allow him to have survived the crash unscathed while taking the life of a decent person, the pilot. "Let's move."

Haunting memories looped through his mind for the next

couple of hours. Along the way, Toby periodically checked for bars. No such luck finding cell coverage out here. It had been too long since the last time he'd visited the national park for him to recall any specifics, like where a ranger station might be. By the time they reached a water source, hunger crept in. If he felt the pangs, Jules must be starving. The term *hangry* applied to his best friend when she was forced to skip a meal.

He couldn't look back at Jules if he wanted to keep his focus, but he heard her as she fell into step behind him. She hadn't spoken since he'd been a jerk toward her earlier. He wished he could go back to being the carefree version of himself that she was used to, but something snapped in his mind when he realized Symes could be the man he'd been searching for over the last five years. Raping and murdering the sister of a US marshal might have been a pinnacle in the bastard's career. The theory had been dismissed by the FBI profiler on the case.

Disgust nearly overwhelmed Toby. What kind of monster would hurt someone as kind and innocent as Lila?

His baby sister was one of the most decent people he'd ever known, along with Jules. Having kind hearts was where the similarities between the two ended.

Toby located a good spot near the water's edge. If they didn't make it out of the desert soon, temperatures would drop. Their clothes were soaked. They would freeze. He needed to figure out a way to start a fire now that the rain had stopped.

Glancing around, he was reminded that everything was wet. Under normal conditions, there was enough material to use for tinder everywhere. Toby always carried a lighter and flint, an old habit from becoming a Boy Scout after his father flaked out on him. His grandmother had signed him up—much to his rebellion—to give him male role models, or so she'd explained.

Toby eventually agreed when he realized he needed to be there for Lila. Having practical survival skills couldn't hurt, and he'd feared that his sick grandmother would be taken from them too soon. Becoming a Scout not only gave him the skills to survive, but it had put him on a straight and narrow path to college for a criminal justice degree and then a career in law enforcement.

Texas had been in a drought, so park rangers would be watching for any signs of smoke, which could play to their advantage. No doubt, there would be a ban on all fire in the park despite the recent rain, which rolled downhill because the ground was too dry and cracked to accept it. Finding a ranger out here could save their lives since they would have better communication devices.

The state needed to be alerted to Symes's escape from custody. If Toby and Jules couldn't recapture Symes, the world needed to be on the lookout.

"They'll be sending out search parties for us by this point," Jules said, breaking the silence that sat between them like pregnant rain clouds.

Toby was thankful she finally spoke up. Could she forgive him for being a jerk? "There's a lot of ground to cover out here."

"True," she concurred. "But it's something."

Darkness blanketed the sky. Toby's eyes had long since adjusted, but it was impossible to see very far. There were no streetlights out here. No roads. In reality, search parties might not pick up until first light.

"My family will receive word and be very worried," Jules pointed out. "They already have enough going on with our grandparents."

She was lucky. No one would miss him.

"Of course your family will be concerned about you," Toby said, mustering as reassuring a voice as he was able. "They love you, Jules." He wanted to add that he loved her too, as a friend. "I'm not going to let anything happen to you." It was a promise both knew he might not be able to keep. "Though, I have a feeling you're the one who will be keeping me alive."

Normally, Jules cracked a smile when he made a statement like that, along with a *damn right* type of remark. This time, she barely nodded when he risked a glance at her.

Jules being mad at him was a rare occurrence. One he disliked with every fiber of his being.

This time, he feared she might never forgive him.

"I'll check over here for more tinder," she said, walking away as she followed the winding riverbed.

Being lost out here meant she had no ability to contact her family or receive updates about her grandparents. Toby didn't mind losing communication with the outside world as much since it wasn't like anyone would stay up all night to wait for word as to whether he was okay or not.

Jules would, an annoying voice in the back of his mind reminded him.

Toby ignored it as he gathered underbrush; the tops were wet but not all of it. He cursed his luck at the timing of the rain. Then again, he could chalk it up to the dark cloud that seemed to follow him around. Even as a teen while working as a lifeguard at the local public pool, a kid had drowned under his watch. Would Jules be safer with another partner on this assignment?

More of that familiar shame cloaked Toby, tightening like a straitjacket around his chest and arms, making it hard to breathe.

Steady wind created a constant white noise in the background, making it impossible to hear where Jules had gone. Toby kept a visual of her in his peripheral. Not only did they have to watch for Symes, but there were other vicious animals that could attack. In the grand scheme of nature, being human could put them at a disadvantage.

Toby had promised to keep Jules safe. He would give his own life in a heartbeat if it meant saving hers.

"Hey," she shouted, her voice echoing. "Toby. Come here. Quick."

A noise like footsteps running sounded to his left.

Was Toby the only one who heard?

Chapter Seven

One look at the stress on Toby's face as he came barreling toward her made Jules realize she'd just scared the hell out of him.

She put both hands up, palms out, in the surrender position. "I didn't mean to freak you out, Toby. I'm good."

Toby halted with the same force as a charging bull in front of a butcher knife instead of a red cape. "It's fine." He panted like he'd just sprinted across a football field. "I just thought that something—"

"I know and I'm sorry," she said, cutting him off before he went down the rabbit hole of imagining something bad happening to either one of them. Being out here as night fell while a killer was on the loose was bad enough. Being here alone was the only thing that could make the situation worse.

His gaze shifted to a spot behind her. It was the reason she'd called him over.

"I haven't checked inside the camper, but it doesn't appear that anyone has been here in a while," she stated, turning around to the green-and-white-striped abandoned camper van. "Looks like someone parked here and then left it."

Toby walked the perimeter of the vehicle, giving it a

wide berth. He leaned in. "There's no smell, which is a good sign." He circled the camper before returning to a spot next to her. "Have you checked the doors to see if they're unlocked?"

"No," Jules admitted, pulling her weapon from her shoulder holster just in case. "But I thought it might make a decent base camp for tonight. Keep us out of the elements and provide safety against wild animals." She couldn't say the same for Symes if he found them. The man was unpredictable. She also realized they might have gone in the wrong direction in their search, because a survivalist like him wouldn't waste an opportunity for free shelter. Would he?

Barely to Toby's right side, she kept her weapon trained on the door as they moved a couple of steps toward it.

Toby reached for the handle with his left hand, turned it and then opened the door. There was no stench of abandoned food or, worse yet, bodies. That was a good sign. Toby stuck his head inside. "Can't see a thing in here."

"Hold on," Jules said, reaching inside his pocket for his phone. She flipped on the flashlight app and moved so close to Toby their arms touched. Under different circumstances, she might notice the trill of electricity shooting up her arm like stray voltage from the point of contact.

Extending her arm until her hand was deep inside the camper, she slowly panned left to right.

"Looks like someone might have left this here for stranded hikers," Toby reasoned. "It's not in bad shape. There's no food, of course. Bears would rip the door off if they got hungry enough. There's a stack of blankets on top of the bed that's pulled out."

A dark thought struck that Symes might be familiar

with this area and, therefore, know about this spot. Anything was possible.

"It seems safe to go inside, and it will keep us from the elements and wildlife," Toby reasoned.

"Will it make us sitting ducks, much like the chopper?" Jules asked. It was impossible not to think about Captain Crawford at the mention of his aircraft. Her chest squeezed.

Toby shrugged. "I hope not." He stepped inside the camper. "Our other option includes using these blankets to pitch a makeshift tent. It won't necessarily keep predators away, but we could insulate ourselves against the elements."

"Seems smarter, though, doesn't it?" she continued. "In case Symes finds this camper. He might expect us to be inside."

"We'd have the element of surprise in our favor," Toby reasoned. "But that won't stop wild hogs from attacking."

Jules sighed. "Or a few others, I'm sure." She stopped to think about it. "Maybe it's best to stay inside the camper tonight and then head out at first light." Searching for Symes in Big Bend National Park was the equivalent of finding a needle in a haystack. Not attempting to find him wasn't an option despite being battered and bruised from the crash. It occurred to Jules the gash on her forehead might not have come from the accident. Symes might have left Toby for dead and smashed her head with a rock.

Would he go back and check? Would he wander far from the relative safety of the chopper?

"Part of me thinks Symes might have slithered away from the chopper far enough to wait us out. Based on our injuries, he might not have expected us to live," she said.

"I thought the same thing, Jules."

"Should we go back? See if he circled around to check on us?" she asked. "We aren't too far away." They would have to climb up rather than make their way down, which could prove a challenge with her knee and Toby's general condition.

"At first light," he said after a thoughtful pause. "We should rest."

Jules had a feeling her pain would only increase.

"Elevating your knee above your heart should help with some of the swelling," he continued as he took a step inside the camper and then offered assistance with his left hand.

As Jules reached out to him, the crack of a bullet echoed through the air. A ping in the camper sounded two inches from her ear.

She immediately dropped to the ground as Toby dived on top of her, covering her with his six-foot-one-inch frame. An instant later, she drew her weapon and aimed at the source of the gunfire.

They were out in the open, exposed. Toby had just risked his life by covering her when he should have slipped inside the camper.

"I don't have a shot," she whispered.

"He's on the move," Toby said. "I can feel it."

"It has to be him," she responded. "Who else would shoot at us without identifying themselves?"

"Toss your weapon toward us," Toby ordered after identifying them as US marshals.

A haunting laugh echoed over them and across the river behind them.

"We need to get around the camper," Jules said. They needed to put some metal between them and Symes. And Symes was the only possibility out here in the middle of nowhere.

"You go first," Toby said as his body tensed, no doubt in pain. With his right hand taped to his body, crushed underneath his heft, the man had to be in excruciating pain. "I'll cover you."

"I got this, Toby," she argued back. He needed more time, and she intended to make sure he got it. Under normal circumstances, she wouldn't hesitate to go first, but she couldn't leave him. His injuries would slow him down.

Another shot fired.

There were only fifteen rounds in her SIG. Two down. Which left thirteen to go. *Too many in the hands of pure evil.*

Symes had thirteen more chances to end one or both of their lives.

Her first thought was that she couldn't lose Toby. Her second was that she couldn't die without seeing her family one more time.

Since she had a finite amount of ammunition, she refused to waste a single bullet. But Symes had given away his location for a few seconds.

"Go," she urged Toby.

With a grunt, he managed to army crawl to safety. He immediately drew his weapon and aimed. "Now you."

Jules sucked in a breath, said a quick prayer she'd learned a bazillion years ago and then crawled toward Toby. Movement made her feel like her head might explode from pain. Her knee pulsed and throbbed to the point she could feel every beat of her heart in it.

Bullet number three fired, hitting its target…*her.*

TOBY RELEASED A string of curses as he fired his weapon to back off Symes. The shot from his left hand got off too late. His reflexes weren't nearly as quick. Now Jules paid the price.

At least he bought her enough time to make it to him.

Immediately, he tucked her behind him. There was no time to assess the damage for himself.

"How bad is it?" he whispered, desperate, as he scanned the darkness for any sign of Symes. They had an escape route, but it was risky.

"I'll live," Jules promised. Could she keep her word?

Toby couldn't lose her. Period.

"We can make a run for the river," he said. "But we have to decide now."

"The river is raging," she pointed out. "I can hear it from here."

They were about twenty-five feet away. "I know, but it'll carry us away from Symes."

Jules hesitated for a moment.

"You're shot and we need to assess the injury, possibly even dress the wound," he said. "I wouldn't normally run in a situation like this, but we can't catch him if he kills us."

"Okay, good point" was all Jules said before she tugged at his good arm.

In a split second, they made a run for it, diving into the chilly water after Toby managed to secure his weapon. With one good arm, he would wear out easily in the frigid water. The cold splash was enough to shock Toby awake.

Temps at night could hover around freezing this time of year, but taking a water route was their best option to escape and regroup.

Toby used his good arm to sluice through the water, keeping as close to Jules as humanly possible.

"My knee already feels better," she said, her voice trembling with cold. "I can already say that much."

"We shouldn't stay in long," he said. Fighting the current to swim to shore was a whole different issue. One they were about to face if they wanted to stay remotely close to Symes.

Toby listened for a splash to indicate Symes had followed them. Instead, he heard an evil laugh that made his skin crawl.

And then it happened. *Splash.*

Never in Toby's thoughts did he imagine Symes would be determined enough to follow them into the water. Symes was roughly twenty seconds behind them, which meant he might be able to catch up to them when they exited the river. The cold water numbed their bodies, which helped with their injuries but would slow their movements.

They needed to find an exit before they froze to death.

"Toby," Jules said with a tone that sent his blood pressure sailing.

"What is it?" he asked. "Are you all right?"

"The blood," she said as he managed to get to her. How on earth he pulled it off with one good arm was anyone's guess. He could thank his Scout survival training that included swimming fully clothed under various conditions. Otherwise, he would be a goner and no help to Jules.

Blood pulsed from the base of her neck on her right side. Her lips were blue, another bad sign. He needed to get her to safety and deal with the wound immediately, if not sooner.

"Stay with me," Toby said to Jules as he slid in behind her. Body to body, she leaned into him. "Put pressure on the wound, Jules."

He could see her eyelids flutter. If she lost consciousness, it was all over. The thought of losing her was a knife stab in the center of his chest.

"I can't lose you, Jules," he whispered. "Keep fighting for my sake. Okay? I wouldn't survive it."

If he had to die on this assignment, he would want it to be with her. If she went, he wanted to go with her. Period.

"Talk to me," he whispered, needing to lock Symes up for the rest of his life before cashing in his chips. "And keep talking."

"Do you remember the first time we met?" she asked, her voice trembling with cold.

Toby would never be able to erase the image of Jules on her first day at the Marshals Service. She walked into the conference room, and his heart thumped double time inside his chest. He'd been certain she would realize his instant attraction to her, but she didn't. In fact, she walked directly toward the seat next to him and introduced herself. The first thing he noticed were her legs. They seemed to go on forever. Up close, though, it was her blue eyes with thick black lashes that smacked him in the chest. Her blond hair with wheat-colored highlights framed a near-perfect Blake Lively look-alike face, complete with a mole under her right eye close to her nose. With her looks, he'd expected a diva, not the down-to-earth, belly-laughing beauty who must have never looked at herself in a mirror. "Remind me."

"You think it was the conference room on my first day at work, but we actually stood in line together a couple of times at Dark Roast Coffee in Austin two months before I ever walked into that room," she said with a smile in her voice. He didn't need to see her face to know when she smiled. He could hear it through the lightness in her tone.

"No way," he countered. "I would have remembered you."

"It was early in the morning, and I had on sunglasses and a baseball cap," she quipped with more enthusiasm in her voice now. "Plus, I was behind you, and you never once looked back." More of that smile came through.

"Doesn't sound like me, even though I do frequent Dark Roast when I'm in the capital," he stated, trying to reach back into his brain for the possibility they'd been in the same room before without him realizing it. There was no way he wouldn't have seen Jules. She was far too beautiful not to notice. "But no way."

"You were deep in what had to be intellectual conversation with a brunette," she said, sounding smug. "I mean, she wouldn't leave your lips alone."

"Do you mean Clingy Carin?" he asked with a laugh that made his ribs hurt. The ever-present danger twenty seconds behind them could be closing in, but Toby couldn't think about that right now.

His focus had to go toward keeping Jules alive and getting them out of this river. The current carried them downstream at an increasing pace. The rush of water sounded ahead, which meant one thing. Waterfall.

Toby couldn't let Jules know about the dangers. *Keep her talking. Figure out a plan.*

Think.

Chapter Eight

Jules was cold. Her teeth chattered. Heavy, wet clothes made lifting her arms to swim even more challenging. Her legs weren't in much better shape. The struggle to stay afloat was real. She had no idea how Toby was pulling it off with one good arm. The man was a force.

Fighting the overwhelming sense of exhaustion, Jules realized she needed to help get them to shore if they were to survive.

She let the Clingy Carin comment go. They could finish this conversation later. It had been a much-needed distraction, but she had to face the fact that if they didn't get out of the water soon, they were going over a waterfall.

Symes was somewhere close behind them too. She didn't risk a backward glance. She was focused on figuring out a way out of this current.

"See the branch coming up?" Toby asked.

"Yes," she said, shivering.

"I want you to grab it," he said. "I'll help push you out of the water. Then I want you to get on solid land."

"You'll be right behind me?"

"Yes," he reassured her as the branch came within reach. "Go."

Jules grabbed hold as she was hoisted out of the water.

She grabbed on for dear life and then immediately searched for Toby. His head had gone under the water.

She frantically searched the surface of the water for him. Nothing. She scanned the area for air bubbles. *Where are you?*

With one hand on her neck to put pressure on her wound and stem the bleeding, she managed to shimmy onto shore like he'd instructed. Knowing Toby, he had a plan. Toby *always* had a plan. It was only a matter of time before his head would surface and he'd pull himself out of the water a little downstream.

Toby, where'd you go?

Jules made it to shore and could kiss the soil, except Toby was still out there, and she still hadn't seen him. Maybe he'd popped his head up for air and she'd missed it while she was shimmying to shore.

Symes was out here too. She searched the shoreline first and then upstream for him. There was no sign of him either. It didn't mean he wouldn't come floating down in another second or two or running down the shore with gun blazing. At last count, he had a maximum of twelve rounds left. Enough to kill Jules and Toby.

Heart pounding, Jules frantically searched for Toby. He meant far too much to her to lose him in this manner.

With a curse, she waded ankle deep into the river. The current was strong, and she feared he might have been swept over the waterfall by this point.

Moving toward the rushing sound, she hopped on her good leg so she could get there faster. Wet clothes hung on her like fifty-pound weights, but nothing would stop her from finding Toby.

She focused her gaze on the water, skimming the surface. Movement on the opposite shore caught her eye. Symes?

No. Not Symes. Toby. He was lying flat on his back. The waterfall was less than ten feet away. Was he alive?

Panic squeezed her chest as she calculated the odds of being able to successfully swim across the current to get to him. She clamped her mouth shut to stop herself from calling out to him. If Symes was in the area, she didn't want to give away their position.

Then again, she would be drawing him to her, not Toby. That might just be a good thing.

Before she could decide, Toby sat up. Even from this distance, she could see his chest heaving for air, but he was alive and that was all that mattered.

He was searching the opposite shoreline, no doubt looking for her.

She waved her free hand in the air to get his attention, resisting the urge to scream his name to tell him that she was safe.

The second he saw her and waved back, relief flooded her. He was alive. She was alive.

The moment of happiness was cut short by the sound of footsteps coming from behind. A quick glance back didn't reveal the threat.

The noise stopped. Was something back there, waiting, biding its time to attack?

Getting to Toby was her first priority as she drew her weapon. Downstream where they were, the river curved and thinned. She signaled for Toby to hike back toward the direction they came. It would be safer to cross at the shortest point in between them.

Toby got the message and signaled he would move upstream. With effort, he managed to stand up. She realized he'd torn the bandage securing his right arm to his body. Was that how he'd managed to keep from drowning?

Now his hand dangled from his broken wrist.

Dizziness set in, but she refused to give in to the urge to lie down and go to sleep. Do that and she might never wake up again.

The footsteps didn't follow. Was that a good or bad sign?

Either way, Jules had to push forward and get to Toby. Could they circle back to the camper to rest? At this point, her body was working off pure adrenaline and probably a shock from the cold. Temperatures had dropped, and she needed to get out of these wet clothes or risk freezing to death. As it was, her teeth chattered. She was certain her lips had turned several shades of blue and purple like when she'd refused to get out of the public pool on a warm day in October. The sun might have been out, but the water had been freezing. She and her brothers, along with their cousins, would beg to stay in the pool until long after the sun went down, and they were close to hypothermia.

They'd eventually been bribed out of the water with the promise of hot cocoa with marshmallows when they got home. Gran Lacy could make a warm drink sound like an adventure.

Jules should be there with her grandma. *Even more reason to keep breathing, kiddo.*

Her thoughts shifted to her father, who'd died far too young. She remembered him as a good man. Her mother had already ditched the family after Dalton was born. Now thirty-two years old, she was the middle child. Her brother Camden was thirty-five years old and the oldest on both sides of the family. Jules was closest in age to her cousin Crystal, who was a year older. Her cousin Duke was thirty years old. Cousin Abilene and brother Dalton were the babies of the family at twenty-eight years old.

Six grandchildren raised by saints, if anyone asked Jules.

Jules had no idea where her mother ended up. She didn't care either. Toby had once asked if she was the least bit curious about the woman who gave birth to her. She'd told him no and meant it. Jules didn't know and didn't care. Or, at least, she'd convinced herself it was true. Every once in a while, though, a question popped into her thoughts. Mostly around birthdays and Christmas. She wondered if her mother ever thought about her. If so, why didn't she reach out and try to communicate? Jules wasn't big on social media like so many of her peers, but she had an account. Couldn't her mother look her up? Send a message? Why hadn't she?

Grandpa Lor, short for Lorenzo, waited until Jules turned thirteen before asking if she wanted more information about her mother. He reassured her in the most loving way that her curiosity would be normal and wasn't any sort of betrayal to those who'd raised her.

Jules had decided to give the subject an evening of thought. She'd tossed and turned over the decision of whether to find out more about her mother. The most burning question, of course, being, why did the woman turn her back on her children?

After a long night with little sleep, Jules decided her mother didn't deserve that much attention. Anyone who decided to raise a child and then abandon them wasn't the kind of person Jules wanted to get to know.

Plus, she had a great childhood on her grandparents' paint-horse ranch. Who got to grow up knowing how much they were loved with siblings and cousins who were like sisters and a brother to Jules? During her teenage years, she witnessed families breaking up, causing trauma to her school friends. She saw them being used as weapons in divorces and hating the fact they would have to spend holidays split up.

Despite the circumstances, Jules never felt ignored or unloved. So, no, she had no reason to find her mother. As far as Jules was concerned, she'd buried the woman years ago. Why resurrect the dead?

Not to mention the simple fact her mother hadn't once sent a birthday card or tried to connect. So, really, why bother losing sleep over someone who didn't want you?

Glancing across the river at Toby, seeing him push forward so they could reconnect, kept her walking when she wanted to fall down. The brain was interesting because it was throwing all kinds of reasons at her to sit down and rest. But she knew that meant she would likely never get back up.

Since she couldn't fathom walking all the way to the spot where the river swerved, she focused on taking one step. Then another. And then one more.

The bend wasn't too far upstream. The threat that had been behind her must have decided she wasn't a good enough meal to attack. Unless it still hunted her, biding its time, waiting.

And then Toby's legs buckled. He landed face-first on the opposite shore.

Forget the bend—Jules had to cross now.

TOBY'S LEGS GAVE OUT, and he bit the dust, so to speak. Forcing himself up on his knees and good hand, he managed to sit back on his heels.

Splashing sounds from the opposite shore sent his pulse racing. What was Jules doing?

Before he could tell her that he was fine, she was in the water and swimming toward him. Thankfully, she'd stemmed the bleeding in her neck. By the time she reached shore, he had to help her out of the water.

One look at her told him exactly where they needed to go. The camper.

With every last ounce of strength Toby had, he helped Jules to the camper. Symes had followed them and, with any luck, gone over the waterfall. Toby didn't want the man to die, because that was too easy an out. He did, however, wish him more pain and a lifetime behind bars.

All Toby had to do was recall crime scene pictures from Lila's murder to find enough anger to fuel his steps back to the camper. "Hang in there, okay?"

"I'm good," Jules promised, forcing every forward step.

They were in the same boat, both depleted by the time they stood two feet in front of the camper's door. The need to find shelter and get out of these wet clothes before they both ended up with hypothermia outweighed the risk of Symes waiting inside. He couldn't be in better shape than the two of them. Would he have made it back first?

Or did he meet his death in the water?

The only positive thing about the second option was that Jules would be safe from the bastard.

With a tentative step forward, Toby gripped the door handle. Much like ripping off a Band-Aid, he swung the door open quickly.

Toby didn't realize he was holding his breath until he sighed in relief. The camper was empty. He helped Jules, who insisted she could manage on her own, inside. If Toby had the energy, he would crack a smile. It was just like Jules to want to stand on her own two feet. Her strength was one of many traits he admired about her. But it was those rare moments of vulnerability that caused him to love her. *As a friend*, he felt the need to remind himself.

"We need to get those clothes off you," he said to her as she leaned against the pullout bed that was probably a dining table and chairs during the daytime. Whoever last left this place realized it would most likely be used to bed down for the night, thus the folded blankets.

Toby dipped his shoulder, letting the backpack drop onto the small kitchenette counter. "What do you need first?"

"Wrap...wrist." Jules was barely hanging on. Her teeth were chattering. Those cold, wet clothes had to come off. *Now.*

"We need to undress you, Jules."

"'Bout time," she said, clearly half-delirious at this point. Normally, he would laugh at a crack like that, but under the circumstances, he was concerned. She wasn't thinking straight.

He locked the door behind them, not sure what good it might do. This place wasn't exactly Fort Knox. A half-decent rock could break a window, and it wouldn't take much strength to force the door open. But it was all they had, so it needed to be enough.

Toby placed his gun on the Formica counter and then placed Jules's next to his. He helped her out of her shoulder holster and then her blouse, forcing his gaze from her full breasts, moving behind her to remove any temptation to stare at her silky skin as her chest rose and fell. He'd unsnapped plenty of bras in his time, so this one shouldn't be a problem. Except he had to use his left hand, which trembled. He'd use the excuse of being cold because it was partly true. But the instant flood of heat and flush of unwelcome arousal kept him honest.

Jules was perfect in every way. From those intense blue eyes to hair that looked like a sun-kissed wheat field. She had curves in all the right places. He was a leg man, and hers didn't disappoint. Though, her full breasts drew his gaze more than once, he was embarrassed to admit.

What could he say? In a physical sense, Jules was like staring at perfection. Add her sense of humor, down-to-earth qualities and the fact she had no idea how beautiful she was, and she was almost too good to be true. Like back in high school when the prettiest, most popular girl took an interest in you.

Toby had been too shy to speak to anyone back then. Too shy or too wounded. It didn't matter. The result was the same. He kept to himself, took care of his baby sister and helped his grandmother as best he could once he got his head on straight.

He wouldn't exactly call himself a Goody Two-Shoes back then. But as a kid who had a lot of responsibility on his plate, he kept his rebellious streak in check. Playing football in high school had made him a champion, given him a college scholarship and a future. Without it, he wouldn't have been able to afford the University of Texas at Austin. He wouldn't have a degree in criminal justice, and he sure as hell wouldn't have a career in law enforcement. He'd been good enough to make the team, but a hotshot quarterback from Kerrville started all four years. Riding the bench had been a blow to his ego back then, but now he realized it had also given him time to study and get a degree.

That all being said, the fact Jules had walked straight over to him on the first day he remembered meeting her in the conference room and sat down was still a miracle. Them being best friends was implausible. Toby didn't open up to people. He preferred to keep to himself.

Jules was the difference. She broke down walls by smiling at you. She made you feel like you were a freakin' god just because she chose the chair next to you to sit down in.

Add her intellect into the mix, and he still couldn't understand why she'd picked him to be her friend.

So, the shaky hand with snapping her bra probably had more to do with a jolt of nerves rather than cold. Cold didn't help matters, though.

He also realized that he needed to keep her talking once he could clear the frog in his throat as her bra hit the floor. "I'm still not sure you're remembering our first meeting right." He would know if she'd been in the same room with him before. Any room.

"I am," she said, her words slurred as he helped her slip out of her slacks. A blue blouse and black slacks had no right looking as sexy as they did on her. They looked even better as piles on the floor.

Hooking her thumb onto her lace-and-silk light pink panties, she took those off next. Need welled up, forming a squall inside Toby's chest.

He couldn't find a blanket to wrap her in fast enough to stop the bomb from detonating inside his chest. He'd be lying if he didn't admit to having the occasional thought of what sex between the two of them would be like. His comebacks had always been immediate. It would blow his mind.

Wrong. That wouldn't even come close. It would wreck him for another woman, body and soul.

And then he would have to face a day when he couldn't have her in his life at all.

Chapter Nine

Jules battled to keep her eyes open. On some level, she understood that if she let them close, they might never open again. Her first thought should probably be how much that would break her family, especially while they dealt with the other crisis. The timing couldn't be worse.

But they weren't the first people who popped into her mind.

Her first thought was Toby. How much he needed her to get through this in case Symes turned out to be the perp behind his sister's brutal murder. How alone he would be without his best friend. How much she couldn't stand the thought of being without him too.

Forget how much her body ached with need when he was this close. Not even her current pain level could completely quash the desire welling inside her.

It also gave her a renewed sense of purpose, so she leaned into it.

After wrapping her in a blanket, Toby attended to her neck wound. The man was beyond amazing, considering he had to use his left hand, ripping open packages with his teeth as he worked quickly and quietly.

"Talk to me, Jules. Tell me about that day."

"You don't think I saw you, but how would I know about

Clingy Carin if I didn't?" she managed to say as her body slowly warmed. Fighting sleep took up the rest of her energy. Talking was easier when her jaw wasn't frozen. The camper might not be much, but it would get them through the night as long as Symes didn't come back for them. His return was a very real possibility that had to be considered.

"Fair point," he admitted as he stripped off his clothes.

Jules immediately cast her gaze down to the pile of clothes on the floor and refocused her attention. She'd been a second too late to avoid seeing a backside so hard she could crack an egg on it. That same backside was also perfectly formed. Those were probably things she shouldn't notice about her best friend. But she couldn't help it. Call it accidental visual contact. Her gaze had been sliding down.

"When I walked into the conference room on my first day, I recognized you immediately," she continued, forcing the words as she opened and closed her mouth a couple of times. She felt like the Tin Man from *The Wizard of Oz*. Too bad there wasn't some kind of magical oil that could get her working again.

If they lived through the night, which was the only possibility she would allow herself to consider, she wanted a large cup of tea and a warm bath.

The naked image of Toby stamped her thoughts. Despite it causing her to use extra energy she couldn't afford to spare, she smiled.

"What's that for?" he managed to ask through a grunt after wrapping himself in a blanket with her help.

"Nothing," she said, clamping her mouth shut. "But you ordered black drip that day and the other time I saw you too."

"You remember my drink?" he asked, moving beside her after draping their garments on counters and chairs to aid in drying, where he took a seat and leaned in. For a split second, it felt sensual, but she realized he was sitting this close for body heat and not because he couldn't stand to be apart any longer.

"Only because it's the same as mine," she said. "And no one goes to a fancy coffee shop to order black coffee when there are caramel macchiatos on the menu, or so it seems."

His laugh was a low rumble from his chest. "I'd say we should lie down, but we can't afford to nod off."

"We have to stay close if we want to keep warm," she said. "Here. Move over here if you can."

Toby did as requested, which had him sitting up and leaning against a wall. This way, they could watch the windows. She managed to scoot in between his thighs, so her back was against his chest. He wrapped an arm around her.

"How's your wrist?"

"Never better," he quipped sarcastically in a tone Toby had mastered.

Feeling his body against hers, along with the rise and fall of his chest, wrapped her in warmth.

Then he whispered, "Being here with you like this is more important than any wrist pain."

He said the words so low that she almost didn't hear them. Except she did. And now she wouldn't be able to erase them from her mind.

They also instantly shifted the mood to the most intimate moment of her life. How could that be? They hadn't held hands, let alone kissed. And yet her body responded like they'd just made out, hot and heavy.

Since being this close to Toby sent heat through her body—which she desperately needed—she didn't move away. She would have under any other circumstance because those words coupled with his arm around her broke down her walls, walls that had been erected out of survival instincts because she couldn't lose her best friend to pursue romance.

Keeping him at arm's length caused its own kind of pain, but it was manageable. Neither discussed their dating life with the other, which kept it neat.

She relaxed, fully exhaling for the first time since this whole ordeal began at the crash. The urge to sleep crept over her like a slow fog inching across the Golden Gate Bridge.

Involuntarily, her eyelids came down.

"Hey, hey, hey." The urgency in Toby's voice cut through, causing her to tense up. "Stay awake. Okay?"

"I'm good," she said, hearing the weakness in her own voice. The momentary boost of energy she got after finding shelter and finally warming up faded. Now her body begged for sleep. He was right, though. She had to stay awake.

Could she?

"I REMEMBER THE first time I saw you," Toby said to Jules. "Every gaze in the room flew to you when you came in."

She shook her head. "Not true."

"Then you weren't in the same conference room I was," he countered, ignoring his own mind-numbing pain. Telling himself that he was fine got him through a whole helluva lot of hard practice sessions in football. He might not have started as QB, but that didn't mean he didn't fully participate in practices. Those sacks racked up in practices and scrimmages. He'd gone in for the starter several times to finish games and receive some time on the clock.

"I was too," Jules said, her words slurring again.

Not a good sign. He needed to keep her awake and talking. At least he'd been able to clean up her wounds and stem the bleeding. Foreheads and necks were bleeders. She'd lost more blood than he was comfortable with, especially since they had no idea how long it would take to be rescued.

No matter how much he hated Symes, Toby wouldn't risk going after the bastard again while Jules was so badly injured. He didn't care about himself, but hurting her to satisfy his revenge was a line he couldn't cross.

Period.

"Did you see Mathers's jaw hit the mahogany table then?" he continued, using the distraction to ease some of his anger at letting Symes get away.

"No," she responded. Her voice had a sleepy quality that shouldn't be sexy. "He hates me."

"Because he can't have you," he pointed out. It was endearing that Jules had no idea every single man with eyes wished they could ask her out.

"Not true," she said, then clarified, "He can't. But that's it."

"Then you explain why every guy stands up when you walk into a room," he said.

"Gentlemen?"

Toby barked out a laugh on that one. "Are you truly that oblivious?"

"What kind of narcissist would I be if I thought every man wanted me when I walked into a room?" she asked.

It was a reasonable question, even if she was off base in her analysis. "Yeah, I get your point there."

"Plus, *you* never wanted me," she said.

Was she delirious?

"That's a lie," he said before he could reel the words in. They needed further explanation. "But I settled on being your best friend so I wouldn't lose you."

"Why do you think you would lose me?" Her breathing slowed, which concerned the hell out of him.

"I'd manage to mess it up between us somehow," he admitted. This wasn't a conversation he'd thought he would ever have with Jules. Not in a million years. Though, to be fair, the words might not have been spoken out loud, but that didn't mean they didn't hang in the air. There were little comments between both of them where he'd picked up hints.

"Why?"

"Because we both know that I'm awful at long-term commitment," he explained. Was he admitting too much? No, he reasoned. Because she wouldn't remember this conversation once she was fully conscious again. This was a rare moment where he could let his guard down and tell her how he really felt.

Well, maybe not admit the full monty. But she deserved to know how much he cared about her. So much so that he wouldn't risk blowing what they had for what might be the best sex of his life.

What if you could go the distance?

Toby quashed the thought. He would royally mess up a relationship with Jules. Besides, she was too good for him anyway. If he didn't push her away, she would still end up hurt. It was the dark cloud that always hovered right above his head. Eventually, everyone he loved would die or be killed. This wasn't a bout of self-pity. It was a reality that he'd learned to accept. And he couldn't bring that curse down on Jules.

"What if it would be different between us?" Jules must not realize what she was saying. She didn't want a relationship with him. She'd been clear about their friendship too.

"I'm sure it would," he finally said after a thoughtful pause. "And that's what scares the hell out of me."

"Toby," Jules started before heaving a sigh that scared him. For a split second, he thought it might be her last.

"Yes, sweetheart," he responded when he realized her pulse was still going strong for the circumstances.

"If I told you that I love you, would that change your mind?" Jules asked with the most vulnerable tone, a tone that brought out all his protective instincts.

As much as he should probably warn her away from a guy like him, he didn't have it inside him to say those words while she was in his arms. Even soaked with river water, her hair had a hint of jasmine scent. Jasmine was his favorite.

"It might," he admitted in a moment of weakness.

"Good," she said. "Remind me never to say those words to you again."

The knife took a second to pull out of the center of his chest. She was right, though. They didn't need to cross that line into real feelings for each other, no matter how strongly his brain put up an argument it would be the best relationship of his life. It also said that they deserved to know the kind of real love, real passion, that would shatter all their walls.

But he couldn't allow himself to go there.

Because losing her would leave him shattered too. And he had no idea how he would ever be able to pick up the pieces again.

"You won't," he whispered. "There's no need to remind you." Once this ordeal was over, she wouldn't likely remember saying any of this. It was weakness talking plus some primal biological urge to bond with someone when circumstances became life and death. So he didn't need to repeat anything said in this camper.

Shame. A growing part of him wanted to throw logic out the window and go for it with Jules. Now that she'd given him an inkling that she might be interested in doing the same thing, his attraction increased tenfold.

Having her in his arms felt like the most perfect thing in the world. Loving her was the easy part. It was as natural as breathing. It was the thought of losing her—and he would—that sucked the air out of the room.

Toby needed to focus on something more productive or risk falling in too deep with his emotions when it came to Jules. There was a point of no return, and he was stepping dangerously close to the line.

He'd been so deep in his own thoughts that he realized Jules had drifted off. Should he let her rest? She was peaceful.

After checking her pulse, he decided it was strong enough to risk letting her get a little sleep.

Plus, he didn't want to move her while her body was against his and the world righted itself for a few moments, moments that would go by in a flash. Once they regained some strength, they could figure out their next move. Even Toby was realistic enough to acknowledge they couldn't continue the search for Symes. At this point, their survival had to come first.

Toby couldn't be certain how long he'd been asleep after he drifted off, but his eyes blinked open the second he heard movement outside the camper.

Instinctively, he sat straight up and scanned his surroundings. Jules didn't move. Not a good sign.

He gently shifted out from underneath her. The threat had to be dealt with first. He quickly dressed and tossed Jules's now-dry garments on the bed.

Grabbing his weapon from the countertop where he'd

left it last night, he palmed it in his left hand. Not having use of his right hand made everything ten times harder.

Moving to the slatted window without making a sound, he searched for a spot where he could take a look at what was outside without the predator realizing it. Make no mistake about it—Symes was every bit as much an apex predator as a mountain lion. If he'd figured out they'd circled back, he planned on hunting them down as prey.

Guess what, jerk wad—no dice. Hell would freeze over before Toby allowed this monster to take another life on his watch.

A deep well of anger swirled low in the pit of his stomach as he looked for the right place to check outside. He refused to give himself away before he was ready. The element of surprise could mean the difference between life and death.

It was quiet. Too quiet out there.

Toby didn't help keep Jules alive last night to let this ordeal end with Symes winning. Could he exit out a window and get the drop on Symes?

Or was he overreacting to a wild boar or deer in search of a morning meal, none the wiser anyone was inside the camper?

An animal would have moved by now. Unless it had killed its prey and was already eating.

Out here, you were either predator or prey. Nature didn't discriminate and it didn't play favorites. Law of survival of the fittest ruled.

Measuring his breath so he didn't make an unnecessary noise, Toby leaned toward the slats of the mini blinds on the door. He might be able to get a peek outside through the small hole where the string wound through to lift the blinds.

Taking in a slow breath and then exhaling just as slowly to calm his racing pulse, Toby found a peephole.

Someone moved.

He couldn't get a good look at the person before they shifted out of view. All he'd seen was a dark-colored shirt. Navy blue or black.

What had Symes been wearing yesterday?

If memory served, he'd been in a prison-orange jumpsuit. Would he have gone back to the chopper to change clothes with Crawford after jumping into the river? Symes would have needed dry clothes to survive the night or risk freezing to death. He hadn't come back to the camper.

Did he believe they would head to the chopper for safety? Or possibly to remove the captain's clothes and use them for their own survival purposes? It sickened Toby to think someone would be capable of such a thing, but he dealt with real scumbags, who raped and pillaged any chance they got. They used any excuse that served them to become the felons they were. Rough childhood? Check. Toby knew a thing or two about being dealt a bad hand. He knew how neglect felt before his grandmother stepped in. And he knew what it was like to lose those he loved.

Didn't make him a criminal.

Or did it?

Hadn't he considered taking Symes down by any means after finding out he might be the bastard who'd killed Lila?

Toby shoved the uncomfortable realization aside. If push came to shove, Toby would do the right thing despite the line being blurred in this case. This was a one-off and didn't define his career.

Besides, there was another piece of information that he hadn't shared with anyone. The perp who'd killed his sister mailed Toby an artifact every year on the anniversary of her murder, taunting him. Even a tame animal came out fighting when injured or cornered.

Before he could get too far down that road, something with the force of a battering ram slammed against the door.

The second hit came before Toby could react.

Jules sucked in a breath, sat up. A look of shock stamped her features. "Toby?"

Afraid couldn't be the way he remembered her.

Chapter Ten

Jules dressed and then scrambled for her 9 mm, which was sitting on top of the counter in between the small metal sink and a two-burner stovetop. "Is he here?"

The third smack into the camper door sent the gun flying across the small space. It slammed against the wall and then tumbled onto the ground.

Standing at the doorway, much to her relief, was a SWAT team.

Jules immediately identified herself and put her hands in the air.

"A ranger passed by this camper at 6:00 a.m. after another located the chopper," a SWAT officer who'd identified himself as Landry Thomas said. His face creased with concern as Jules stumbled backward before tripping on the bed. Getting up too fast had been a mistake.

"Help is here," Landry said to them.

Toby sat down as relief seemed to buckle his knees.

They were safe. Help had arrived.

"What about Symes?" Toby immediately asked.

Landry shrugged. "I'm sorry. He hasn't been apprehended as of yet. Rest assured we have a lot of manpower on this one. No one wants this monster to roam around free."

Those were the last words Jules remembered hearing before she blacked out.

WAKING UP TO the sounds of beeping machines and no sign of Toby caused Jules to sit up and spam the nurse's call button.

A short, squat nurse in scrubs with a kind face and spiky hair came running into the room. "Everything all right in here?"

"I'm, um… No," Jules said, still disoriented and woozy. She recognized the feeling of pain medication because she'd been in scrapes before that landed her in the hospital. Nothing to this degree but enough to have to take the occasional pill. "I'm fine. I think." She glanced around, blinking to bring water to her dry eyes. "My partner is—"

"In the next room," the nurse said as she moved to Jules's side.

"How is he? How's Toby?"

"I'm Pamela, by the way. And right now, I'm more concerned with how you're doing." She went about checking dials and reading monitors.

Jules didn't like the nurse evading the question about Toby. Her pulse kicked up a few notches, as evidenced by the beeping machine beside her bed. She threw covers off and reached for her IV, ready to yank it out.

"Hold on there," Pamela soothed. "HIPAA laws prevent me from discussing another patient's condition with non-family members." The nurse shot a warning look at Jules. "However, if I could say anything, I would reassure you that your partner is still under sedation but came through surgery fine. His wrist has been set."

"Surgery?" Oh, no. How badly had Toby been injured? What did that mean?

"If you promise not to rip out your IV, I'll grab a wheelchair and take you for a 'walk' so you can see for yourself."

Pamela stood there like a mother who'd just scolded a two-year-old for throwing a temper tantrum.

"I'll wait right here," Jules said.

"Good," Pamela fired back. She seemed spunky and came across as someone you didn't want to have angry at you. "We can talk about how you're doing on our stroll."

"Deal," Jules said. She would have promised anything to be able to see how Toby was doing with her own eyes.

Pamela disappeared, returning not two minutes later with a wheelchair. "We'll have to untangle you from a couple of monitors, but the IV comes with us. I can hook it here." She pointed to a metal bar coming up from the back of the wheelchair. Jules didn't care how the nurse got her on the move. All she cared about was seeing Toby and knowing he would pull through.

For a split second, she thought about Symes.

"Do you know if an escaped rapist has been recovered?" she asked the nurse, figuring the recapture would make national news.

Pamela frowned as she shook her head. "I'm afraid not. Your boss has been stopping by, asking the nursing staff to take the best possible care of both of you. I got nosy and asked around, found out why you are here. You and your partner are lucky to be alive, from what I've heard."

"Stories like these get blown out of proportion," Jules said.

"Your family has been calling on the hour too," Pamela said. "The attention you've gotten in here made us wonder if you were some kind of celebrity." Pamela paused. "Turns out, you two are actual heroes, not just overhyped Hollywood types."

As much as Jules appreciated the sentiment, all she could think about right now was making sure Toby was alive and going to be fine.

"Why was my partner in surgery?" Jules asked, then added, "Hypothetically."

"It would have been from shrapnel from a door splintering off and spearing him below the rib cage on his right side," Pamela whispered as she helped Jules into the chair.

After a couple of minutes of tinkering that felt like hours, they were on the move.

Jules's heart pounded the inside of her chest as she was wheeled out of her room and into the next. The blinds were drawn. The curtains closed. More of those annoying beeps sounded. Except there was an element of comfort to them in Toby's room because it meant his heart was beating just fine.

"Push me closer so I can see him?" Jules asked. The nurse had stopped after taking two steps inside the room. She needed to see him first. Then she would call her family to let them know she was awake and fine.

Pamela complied. "I'll leave you two alone for a few minutes."

"Thank you," Jules said as she waited for the nurse to exit before wheeling herself to Toby's bed. His was closest to the window, where it was darkest.

Seeing him calmed her pulse a few notches. Knowing he would be okay helped. Being here with him was nothing short of a miracle.

Jules drew a blank on how they'd ended up in the hospital. The last thing she remembered was Landry telling her Symes hadn't been recaptured.

She reached over to touch Toby's hand through the metal bars of his hospital bed, where he was flat on his back. The familiar jolt of electricity at the point of contact provided comfort. Did it mean he was still vibrant? Alive? That she was? That their connection was as strong as ever?

Resisting the urge to pull her hand away, she entwined their fingers and rested her head on the cold metal.

"Time's up," the nurse said, returning after several minutes passed without a hint of movement from Toby other than the beeping machines reassuring her that his heart was still beating.

"Mind if I stay a little while longer?" Jules asked.

"You should get back to—"

"Please," Jules cut in. "My partner means the world to me, and I want to be here when he opens his eyes in case he's disoriented."

"That might be a while," Pamela said softly.

"Any chance I can have my room changed to the spare bed in this room?" Jules continued, figuring you didn't get what you didn't ask for. Besides, all anyone could ever tell you was no, and then you'd be right back where you started. No harm done.

"I'll see if that can be arranged, but I can't make any promises," Pamela said in a moment of compassion as she walked out.

"Thank you," Jules said from the bottom of her heart. She couldn't imagine being taken away from Toby while he was heavily sedated. They'd already lost Symes, who could be targeting his next victim by now, for all she knew. If she wasn't so woozy and tired, frustration would nail her. At this point, she didn't have the energy.

We aren't the only ones who want him to be caught.

There were multiple agencies with feet on the ground and eyes in the sky tracking Symes. Good news could come any minute.

Eleven years.

The reminder he'd evaded arrest for eleven years slammed into her as if she'd run full force into a brick wall. At least now, law enforcement had a general idea of his location. Besides, he might have died in the river after jumping in to follow them. He could have gone over the edge of the waterfall. His body might not show up for days or weeks.

He might already be dead.

If not, Toby wouldn't be able to let the case go. Especially not after the realization Symes could have been his sister's killer.

Jules battled the urge to close her eyes again. She wanted to be wide-awake when Toby opened his.

Minutes ticked by. Before she knew it, an hour had slipped past.

Pamela returned, knocking softly at the door before entering, as though the room was sacred space. It was to Jules.

"You should probably go back to your room to eat," Pamela urged in a quiet, almost reverent tone.

Jules lifted her head long enough to shake it.

"I thought that might be your stance," Pamela said. She stepped into the hallway for a few seconds before returning with a tray of food. "Let's get you set up." Pamela grabbed the tray table from the next bed after setting the food on top.

This time, Jules nodded. She wasn't hungry. Nor could she think about eating while Toby was still in this condition. Pain medication always affected her stomach too, so there was that. But arguing with a determined-looking Pamela would be counterproductive.

"I'll check on you in a few minutes, okay?" Pamela's question was rhetorical. The nurse was coming back. The fact she cared about her patients came through in her tone. "There's water in the white jug with a straw, but I can bring you a Coke or juice if you'd rather."

"Water's good." Jules studied the nurse for a few seconds. "Thank you, Pamela."

Those words netted a genuine smile from an otherwise concerned face. "You're welcome." She started toward the door and then stopped a few steps short. "I know you're worried about your partner, and it's obvious to anyone paying attention you have a special bond. I can't help thinking that he would want you to eat something."

Jules cracked a melancholy smile. "He would get on my backside if I didn't at least try."

"So you will?" Pamela pressed. "For him?"

"Yes," Jules said, picking up the burger that didn't look half bad. "For him."

"Good" was all Pamela said before exiting the room.

Before Jules could get the burger to her mouth, Toby cleared his throat.

"You gonna share that burger?" he asked. His voice was the closest to heaven she'd ever been.

"Do you want a bite?" she asked, smiling a genuine smile this time.

"Water first," he croaked with an attempt to smile back. He winced instead.

"Take it easy there, Ward. Can't have you busting another rib," Jules joked.

Toby gave her a look. He was famous for being able to communicate paragraphs with one of his signature glances.

Rather than try to get up, Jules just gave Toby her water jug. The thing was gigantic, and she was sure an IV had already given her plenty of fluids. He could take down the entire jug.

After taking a sip, his expression turned serious. He wanted to know about Symes.

Jules shook her head. She didn't have the heart to say the words out loud. Symes escaping would haunt her until the man was recaptured without any additional lives lost. Anything less and she would never be able to forgive herself.

Toby's gaze intensified as he stared at the closed mini blinds behind her. A muscle in his jaw ticked. "Have you spoken to Mack?" Herbert Mackenzie was their supervisor.

"No," she admitted, offering her burger.

"I was joking before," Toby said. "You eat it."

Jules took a bite and then chewed. "I was waiting for you to wake up before I contacted Mack. Didn't want to leave your side."

"How long have I been out?" Toby asked.

"I woke up a few hours ago," she said. "I'd have to ask the nurse to be certain, but you were in surgery, and I was next door at least twenty-four hours."

Toby searched around the nightstand next to him, along with the tray table. "Have you seen my phone?"

"No," she admitted. "Haven't thought about either of our phones, to be honest. My biggest concern was making sure you woke up."

He reached for her hand and then squeezed before finding the button that made his bed move to sitting. Any movement caused him to wince. Then he took inventory of his physical condition. "I look like I've been through hell."

"We both have," she said, mustering an empty smile before taking another bite. Now that he was awake, her stomach decided it could take down some food. "Do you want a french fry?"

"Do you think they just call them 'fries' in France?" Toby quipped, some of his usual easygoing sense of humor returning.

"Oh, Mr. Funny, coming back with the witty comments already?" she teased, trying to lighten the intense mood.

"Gotta do my part to keep you on your toes, Remington," he fired right back. At least they were going through the motions, pretending that both of their lives hadn't just been devastated. "How did your family take the news?"

"Haven't talked to them yet," she admitted. "All I could think of was my partner."

"I'm honored," Toby quipped with a dramatic gesture, that all-too-familiar wall coming up between them. He picked up a couple of fries and popped them in his mouth.

"Good. You should be," Jules shot back. Their usual lighthearted banter felt hollow now. Those conversations had lifted their spirits during rough times but couldn't make a dent now.

"How are you doing, Jules?" He caught her gaze and held it. A moment of vulnerability crossed his features. "Be honest."

"I feel like I've been in a car crash with no seat belt," she said. "Not to mention the prisoner I was sitting on got away, now able to maim, rape and murder, while I'm trying to choke down a burger in a hospital while my best friend comes out of surgery. So, yeah, pretty crappy."

"Yeah, I figured." Leave it to Toby to see through her fake smile. He frowned. "Same here. What are we going to do about it?"

Chapter Eleven

Jules was already shaking her head before Toby finished his sentence.

"What do you mean, 'What are we going to do about it?'" Jules asked, looking incredulous as she studied him. "You're going to heal, and we're going to let our colleagues catch this bastard."

For a hot second, Toby debated telling her that hell would freeze over before he stayed in a hospital bed while Symes roamed free. What good would it do? Jules would worry. She would try to keep a better eye on him so he didn't slip out and go off half-cocked after Symes.

"We're on medical leave from work," Jules continued with a heavy dose of shock mixed with anger in her voice. Because she knew him well enough to know that he wouldn't be able to let this go. "We're both going to take a step back, Toby. Because our jobs would be on the line. And we wouldn't just be insubordinate if we attempted to arrest Symes on our own, and, heaven forbid, he ended up dead. We'd be under investigation. The possible link to your sister's murder would come up, and then we would be on the wrong side of the courtroom, needing a defense attorney. Is that what you want?"

"No, of course not," he admitted. Jules made good points.

"And if that doesn't convince you of what a bad idea

going after Symes unauthorized would be, how about the fact that neither one of us is operating at half speed, let alone full speed," she pointed out. "That's not exactly operating on a level playing field, is it?"

All the logic in the world wouldn't stop him from wanting to be the one to catch Symes and ensure justice was served. As stubborn as Toby could be, he'd never been unprofessional or reckless. He took wearing a badge seriously and understood the responsibility that came along with the job.

Could he step away?

One glance at the bandage just below his ribs, the soft cast on his right wrist and the rest of his injuries said he needed to listen to his friend and trust the system to work. If, once he was healed enough to go back to work, Symes was still at large, Toby could put in a request to be assigned to apprehend the bastard.

He heaved a sigh that hurt like hell as he exhaled. Were his ribs cracked too?

"You're right, Jules."

She blinked a couple of times, clearly stunned at his about-face. "Hold on. Say that again."

He shot her a look. "You heard me."

"Did I, though?" she asked with a smug look on her face.

"You're right," he conceded. "You made a helluva lot of sense just now." He grabbed another fry, chewed and swallowed it, along with his pride. "The best course of action is to heal and follow protocol."

"I'm glad you see it that way, Toby," she said, all signs of smugness gone now. "Because I honestly didn't think I'd get through to you."

"You have my word," he confirmed.

You're the only one who could, Jules.

"Am I that stubborn?" he asked, grabbing a few more fries.

"Do bulls have horns?"

Logic said he had to walk away from the case. Could he keep his emotions in check enough to follow through with his promise?

"ARE YOU SURE they should be releasing you from the hospital so soon?" Jules's question brought a smile to Toby's face.

She'd insisted the nurse move all her belongings to the bed next to Toby so they could share a room.

"*You're* being released," he countered.

"I didn't have surgery twelve hours ago," she said with a cocked eyebrow.

He motioned toward the machine loudly beeping his heartbeats. "No one gets rest inside a hospital. They've done everything they can for me, and I'm out of the woods. There's no point in keeping me here, running up the bill."

Jules bit down on her bottom lip—a lip he shouldn't find mesmerizing considering their friendship status.

"I guess that makes sense," she reasoned. "Then it's settled."

"What is?" he asked.

"You're coming home with me," she stated.

"I hate to point out the obvious, but you're not in much better shape," he said on a chuckle that hurt like hell. It felt like a baseball bat had been taken to his ribs.

Jules clamped her mouth shut. Whatever snappy comeback she had died on her tongue. "At least we'll be able to keep each other company."

Toby nodded. Part of him needed Jules to know why he hated Lila's murderer from the deep recesses of his soul. "He mails me mementos every year on the anniversary of her murder."

Jules's expression softened. "What kind of animal would do that?"

"The theory about Lila being a feather in this bastard's cap developed after I called in the FBI to handle the evidence," he explained.

"I'm so sorry, Toby," she said with so much compassion that he wanted to reach out and take her in his arms, forget the past. He wished he could do just that…forget. But Symes, if he was the perp after all, refused to let Toby move on.

"He taunts you," she said. "Which is all the more reason not to play into his hands."

"Sounds logical," he admitted. "Would you be able to walk away?"

"I can't begin to know what I would do if I was in your shoes. Honestly. I can't imagine a worse hell. I just wish you'd told me all this before."

"Why?" he asked. "What would that have done?"

"You wouldn't have had to go through it alone," she said. "I could have supported you better." She shook her head. "I could have been a better friend."

"Impossible," he shot back. "You've always been a great friend." Why did the word *friend* sound so hollow now?

Did Toby really want to know the answer to that question?

He decided the topic was better left alone.

Before he could ask about her family now that they were on the subject, Herbert Mackenzie—aka Mack or Sherbert, depending on their mood—walked in.

"You haven't returned my calls," Herbert said to Toby after a perfunctory greeting to Jules. Their supervisor pulled up a chair in between their beds. Being in a hospital gown while meeting with his boss was just about the most awkward thing Toby had experienced to date. Thankfully, he wasn't standing up with his backside to the door when Mack walked in, or they both would have a reason to be embarrassed.

"No, sir," Toby said.

"There a reason you decided not to check in with me?" Mack asked.

"No, sir," Toby repeated.

"Good," Mack said. "Because I've been worried about two of the best marshals my district has ever seen."

"We're being released," Toby said.

Mack's gaze shifted to Jules for confirmation. She nodded.

"Sounds like good news," Mack said. He was middle-aged with a potbelly and a comb-over. But the man was tough as nails when he needed to be and could outrun half the sprinters Toby had ever met. You'd never find a better person to have your back. "You look like hell, though. Is releasing you a good idea?" A small bit of humor creeped out of their normally stern-faced supervisor.

"That's what I said," Jules piped in.

"You two planning to team up on me all night?" Toby quipped.

"We can't," Jules shot back. "You're being released, remember?"

Mack chuckled as he leaned forward, clasping his hands. A couple of seconds passed before his expression morphed back to its usual state: serious.

"I could have lost both of you," he said with a heavy voice.

"We made it," Jules reassured him.

"Comms didn't go out on the flight by accident," Mack informed them. "I'm not sure how we got lucky and the two of you survived, but I don't intend to let anything like this ever happen again."

"You couldn't have known the chopper would go down," Jules said.

"The site is still being investigated, but foul play is suspected," Mack told them. Toby caught on the second Mack said comms had been tinkered with.

Jules muttered the same curse Toby was thinking.

"Was someone on the inside involved?" Toby asked. "Captain Crawford?" As much as he wanted to respect the deceased, it was a fair question.

Mack shrugged. "The only thing I know for certain is that I won't rest until I have answers."

Having someone cover Symes's tracks from the inside could be how he'd escaped capture for eleven years. No one said it outright, but the others had to be thinking it at this point.

"You'll keep us informed," Toby said.

Mack nodded. "Here's the thing. You two were aboard, so someone will be coming to speak to you too."

"As in, we were part of this?" Toby said.

"Someone in the Bureau noticed Symes had a tattoo similar to the one in your sister's case," Mack stated.

"And this person thinks I would risk the lives of two innocent people to kill Symes when I could just slit his throat instead?" Toby didn't hide his disgust.

"Accountability," Mack said. "That's the theory being bantered around." He held a hand up. "It's unbelievable, but we need to take all theories under consideration. Becoming defensive will only make our office look like we have something to hide."

"We don't," Toby felt the need to confirm, even though

nothing in Mack's body language or expression said he needed the reassurance.

"Goes without saying," Mack said.

"Does this mean the agency investigating believes that I'm somehow involved?" Jules asked.

"Guilty by association?" Toby added. He could see how an investigator who didn't know either of them from Adam might draw a conclusion that Jules would do anything to help Toby without taking into account her character. Because if the investigator knew her personally, they would realize she would never willingly break the law. She would argue and fight until her last breath to stop him from doing something that could hurt him in the long run or end his career. And then she would walk away.

"I've given my statement endorsing your innocence, covering all bases," Mack stated. "It's no secret the two of you are close friends."

"Which means people will suspect me too," Jules said, coming to the same conclusion.

The realization that Toby could in no way, shape or form go after Symes without implicating Jules struck like a sledgehammer to the center of his chest. His actions would reflect on her. He'd come to the understanding that he couldn't go after Symes earlier. The point was being hammered home with this conversation. The new development that his actions would be under a microscope slammed into him.

Being treated like a criminal didn't sit well.

"Jules's name shouldn't be associated with mine," he said. "Period." Causing his best friend to come under scrutiny when she was innocent made his good hand fist.

"You know how these things go," Mack said, sounding just as defeated. "We have to let this run its course."

Toby did know. The fact frustrated him to no end when Symes was the one out there raping and murdering.

"He's been taunting you for years, Toby," Mack said, taking his tone down to a more personal level. "You've cooperated. Turned over evidence. But anyone who puts themselves in your position doesn't come up on the good side of the law if they get a chance to avenge their sister's murder. It's as simple as that."

Toby understood more than he wanted to admit. Learning Symes could possibly be connected to his sister caused him to see red.

"If I'm completely honest, I could have crossed a line in the heat of the moment if I'd been given the chance," he said to his boss. "Jules wouldn't have allowed it. She talked me off the ledge and tried to force me to see reason when I was blinded by revenge." Even more reason she shouldn't have to come under scrutiny. Because he also realized investigators could nitpick someone's career to death. Possibly even find a small infraction that would be brought to light, examined and possibly used against Jules at a later date.

"You would have done the same for me," Jules said.

"Since the two of you are under investigation, you won't be able to work any assignments together for a while," Mack said, bringing the conversation back on track.

"Understandable," Jules said.

"Still isn't fair," Toby added.

"Maybe not," Mack said. "But I have every intention of protecting you both to the best of my ability. If that means you aren't in the office on the same days, so be it."

"What about our personal time?" Jules asked.

The question hit Toby hard, even though he understood her need to separate herself from him.

"You can do whatever you want on your own time,"

Mack stated. "I have no jurisdiction there." He paused, then issued a sharp sigh. "Neither of you deserve the scrutiny you're about to be under. That's what I wanted to come down here and tell you personally. But I have to follow protocol and allow the investigation."

"Okay," she said.

Mack turned to Jules. "Your leave begins as soon as you're cleared from medical. I don't want you coming back to work until your grandparents are better."

Toby didn't know how he would get through any of this without Jules. But he was a cement block tied around her neck. He couldn't let himself drag her to the ocean floor along with himself, no matter how much it hurt to do any of this without her.

Chapter Twelve

Mack explained that he had someone waiting outside to take them home before excusing himself and ambling out of the hospital room. As he exited, a flurry of activity began as part of the patient release process. Jules gave her electronic signature several times before being cleared to get dressed. She slipped into dirty clothes, wishing she had something clean to wear.

While Toby dressed—with help that he grumbled about—Jules provided an update to her family in their group chat. She was too tired to explain everything but reassured everyone that she was okay and that she was cleared to head home.

There'd been no change with her grandparents, so not a lot of updates there. Jules would head home, get a night or two of rest and then pack up to head back to Mesa Point so she could take her turn watching over their beloved grandparents.

Toby hadn't said two words to her since Mack left. She was beginning to worry that he planned to shut her out.

"Ready?" she asked her friend, figuring they could talk through whatever caused him to close up on her during the long car ride to her house.

"I'll figure out my own ride," he said, dismissing her with his tone.

"Hold on a minute," Jules said. "What's that all about?"

"You're better off without me," he said, almost so low she didn't hear him.

"Get your stuff and let's go," she said with the voice she used when there was no room for argument.

Nurses arrived with wheelchairs when tension was about to bubble over.

"We're here to spring you out of jail," one of the nurses said with a little more cheer than the situation called for. Talk about not being able to read the room.

Toby mumbled something that Jules couldn't quite pick up and didn't dare ask about. He didn't put up an argument. She'd learned when to be quiet when it came to her friend.

Once they were out of the hospital and safely tucked inside the back of an SUV with blacked-out windows, she spoke to the driver. "We're going to my town house." She rattled off the address.

Toby started to protest, so she reached over and touched his forearm. He clamped his mouth closed, settled low in the seat and closed his eyes.

"Does this mean we aren't talking anymore?" she asked.

"You're better off without me," he repeated.

"Is that really what you think, Toby? Because that hurts."

"I'm hurting you, Jules. Being my friend is bad for you and your career." He didn't look at her. Instead, he turned to face the window.

"Your friendship is one of the best things that ever happened to me," she said, trying to keep her emotions in check. "Plus, we'll get through this investigation because neither one of us did anything wrong. It's absurd anyone would think we would intentionally damage the chopper, if for no other reason than the fact we care about each other."

Toby didn't speak, which was a good sign this time.

"Besides, what kind of person would I be if I ducked out on you now?" she asked.

"A smart one," he said quietly.

"If the situation were reversed, would you be able to turn your back on me?"

"Not the same thing, Jules."

"Really?" she asked. "Because it looks the same to me."

"You have every reason to live, Jules. You have a family who would miss you if you were gone," he pointed out. "I have nothing. No one."

"What are you talking about?" she asked. "You have me."

"I'm jeopardizing you," he stated. "If you were smart, you'd cut bait and run."

"Let's say, for argument's sake, that I'm not smart," she countered. "What happens then? Are you going to shut me out?"

Toby was quiet for a long moment. Then came, "You know I can't do that."

"Then don't do it now," she said. "Talk to me. Lean on me. Let me help."

"What if it drags you down?"

"Then I'll deal with that," she said. She had no intention of allowing him to go through this ordeal alone. "You don't deserve any of this either. Surely you see that."

He nodded without a whole lot of enthusiasm.

"Let's get to my house and try to rest," she said. "If you're not with me, I'll worry about you. So we might as well stick together at this point."

"Wrong conclusions could be drawn if we're noticed together," he said.

"Do you think I care about what other people think?" She didn't.

"Maybe you should, Jules. We're talking criminal charges if this thing goes south," he said.

"You're not a criminal, Toby," she said. "You don't deserve to be treated like one."

"Knowing that I'm under investigation makes me want to find him, Jules."

"I had the same thought," she said. "Part of me wants to do something to prove our innocence and right the situation again. If we hadn't lost him, we wouldn't be in this predicament."

"No, we wouldn't."

"But we have to trust the justice system will work for us too," she said. "If we don't, our badges do us no good."

"Damn," he said. "I hate when you're right."

"What did you say?" she teased, thankful that she'd been able to break through his walls even just a little. Was it enough?

Time would tell.

TOBY WASN'T SURE how long he'd been asleep by the time the SUV pulled up in front of Jules's town house. The first ray of sunlight peeked across the landscape. Jules lived in a cul-de-sac in a small community northwest of San Antonio as her primary address. However, she traveled most of the time for her job, same as him, so she was barely home long enough to enjoy her two-story town house.

"Hey," he said quietly to the sleeping beauty next to him.

Jules sat up with a start. Sucked in a breath as her gaze darted around. Her being on edge was no doubt the result of what they'd been through in the last forty-eight hours, give or take. The effects could last days or weeks.

"You're fine," he reassured her. He knew better than to

touch her until she got her bearings, or he might end up with an elbow jab to the face.

"Toby?" she asked, but the question was rhetorical. He hated how small and vulnerable her voice sounded.

"Right here, Jules," he soothed. "I'm here."

"I fell asleep," she stated as she figured out where she was and how she got here.

"We're home," he said. "Let's get out and get you to bed."

"Nice try, Toby," she quipped. Her sense of humor returning was a good sign.

The driver parked as close to her front door as possible. He exited the vehicle and helped her out first, shouldering her backpack before leading her to the front door. Toby could walk to the door on his own. He didn't need anyone's help.

He exited the vehicle, wanting to be the one who helped Jules inside.

He'd slept most of the ride, waking on and off. He did some of his best thinking in the in between sleep and awake state while he powered down and recharged his battery.

The investigation made sense from an outsider's point of view. If he could set aside the fact he was involved and knew he was innocent, it made sense for an agency to question the motivation of everyone involved. Captain Crawford had died. The man didn't deserve his fate. So, yeah, Toby could set aside his own personal frustration at being treated like a criminal when he thought about a spouse losing a partner or a child losing a father.

Toby wasn't upset about the investigation as much as the reality Symes had bested him. The man had gotten away. Why the hell would karma be on a murderer's side?

That was one of many questions that would most likely never be answered in his lifetime, despite his fundamental belief that the good guys almost always won.

Following Jules and the driver inside, Toby realized he'd been in his own world, forgetting to ask the driver his name. He rectified the situation immediately by putting out his hand and introducing himself to the six-foot-two-inch driver, who looked like he could start for the Dallas Cowboys on the defensive line.

"Rick Dane," the driver said, taking the offering and returning a firm shake. "It's an honor to be your driver today, sir."

"Call me Toby," he instructed, offering to take the back-pack.

Rick shook his head. "Sorry, si…Toby. The boss gave explicit instructions for me to take care of any bags. This is all you have between the two of you."

"I got it now," Jules stated.

Rick made a motion to set it onto the table in the hall-way instead. "Okay?"

"Of course," Jules said, ever the diplomat.

"Is there anything else either of you need before I leave?" Rick asked.

"No, thank you," Jules stated. "We have phone apps for food delivery. I put in an order that should be delivered sometime in the next hour on the way home and tacos too."

Toby gave her a look. "When did that happen?"

"While you were asleep," she said before turning back to Rick. "We have everything we need. Thank you for get-ting us home safely."

"You're welcome," Rick said. Toby was happy the man didn't say *my pleasure*, as so many had started saying. He liked a simple *you're welcome* because he knew that—most of the time, at least—no employee making fifteen dollars an hour or less was all that pleased serving fast food, no matter how good the nuggets might be. *You're welcome* was more honest, if anyone asked him.

After walking Rick to the door to personally thank him, Toby turned to Jules. "How are you doing really?"

"Honestly?" she asked. "All I want is a shower and clean clothes."

"Go do it," he said. "I'll handle deliveries."

"Are you sure?" she asked. "You must want the same things."

"We'll go in turns in case food shows up," he said.

"Here, take my phone," she offered. "I'll unlock the screen so you don't have to worry about a password."

He cocked an eyebrow, unsure if he wanted any personal messages popping up while it was in his charge. "You sure about that?"

"Don't be weird," she said, holding it out on the flat of her palm. "Take it."

Toby did, noticing the familiar jolt of electricity that came with making skin-to-skin contact with Jules.

"And don't read my personal texts," she stated with a whole lot of attitude.

"Wouldn't dream of it," he said with dramatic flair. "I'll just be on the couch."

"Um, hold on," she said, running upstairs and down in a matter of a few seconds. "You left these clothes after we got caught in the mud hiking and had to strip down."

"Hey, I used my spare joggers that I always keep in the back of my vehicle," he argued.

"Shame," she said with another one of those smiles that caused a knot to form inside his chest. "But these will come in handy after you shower." He noticed the clothes were folded on top of a beach towel.

"Use the towel so you don't get all that gunk from your clothes on my new couch," she said.

"Got it, Sarge," he quipped. He would salute if his right hand wasn't in a sling and his left full of her cell, along with the pile she'd just placed on top. "And thanks for washing my clothes." He managed to drop the bundle onto the couch without it spilling over. Next, he pulled out the beach towel and draped it over the cream fabric. "Happy now?"

"You know I am," she said before heading back upstairs.

Jules's two-level town house had a sitting area almost immediately after you walked in the door. The L-shaped sofa was new and looked like something he could really sink into. A flat-screen TV had been mounted over the fireplace. He should know how difficult it had been to install considering he'd done it himself. Even looking at it now, his chest puffed out at the good job he'd done. Bonus? He'd shaved off installation costs for Jules.

The all-white kitchen had a farm sink and stainless-steel appliances. The white marble island had a couple of bar chairs tucked into one side.

In the next hour and a half, the fridge was full, and they were both showered and in clean clothes.

"Are you hungry?" Jules asked as he joined her at the kitchen table.

"Some," he admitted. He refused to take more medication than absolutely necessary, and the pain kept his appetite at bay.

"Breakfast tacos should be arriving any minute," Jules said. "From that little place you love."

"In that case, I'm starving," he said.

A notification on her app dinged. She checked the screen. "He's pulling up right now."

"I got this." Toby met the driver on the front porch.

Jules had an end unit in the big cul-de-sac that came complete with her own garage. The place had the feel of a small European village with iron gates and cobblestoned streets.

He greeted the driver, took the bags and inhaled the scent of bacon and eggs wrapped in a tortilla. Chopped red onions and cilantro made his mouth water. As it turned out, he was hungry for the right meal. Jules knew him better than anyone.

Back inside, he locked the door behind him before joining her at the table, where she'd set two places. The food was gone in a matter of minutes. He polished off a glass of water, thought about coffee, then decided against it. Despite sleeping for most of the ride down, he was bone-tired and suspected Jules was too.

"I should probably go to bed, but my mind won't stop spinning," she said after he helped clear the table and load the dishwasher. "I'm afraid I'll have another nightmare."

"What about TV?" he offered, motioning toward the couch. "We could put on a movie."

She nodded and then located the remote to close the blinds. The things were a miracle because they could block out almost all sunlight with a push of a button.

"Sit on my good side," he said, sinking into the sofa. His shoes were off, so he put his feet up on the marble coffee table.

After tapping the screen of the remote a few more times, the TV came to life and a menu loaded.

"What are you in the mood for?" she asked.

"Definitely not a comedy," he said on a chuckle and was reminded just what a bad idea that was. His wound wouldn't let him forget that any movement greater than breathing would be punished.

"Got it," she quipped. "*Old Yeller* it is."

"Why not put on *Hachi* as a double feature?" he shot back.

"Only if we can watch *Marley & Me* after," she continued.

"Great," he said. "Did you think to bring a box of tissues with you?"

Jules laughed and it was about the best sound he'd ever heard. "Okay, how about a documentary on quarterbacks from a couple seasons ago."

"You know I won't put up an argument," he agreed. "Is that what you want to watch?"

"I don't mind," she said. "Besides, it'll be a good distraction." She put the remote down after setting the volume at a reasonable level and then curled into the crook of his left arm before reaching for the blanket she kept on the sofa and covering them both with it. She rested her head close to his. "I can hear your heartbeat. Good to know it's still beating strong."

He could hear it too. It was Jules. She made his pulse race. He was just normally better at hiding the fact.

Within a matter of minutes, her steady, even breathing told him that she'd fallen asleep. So he relaxed too. Before he knew it, he was out.

A thud coming from upstairs shocked Toby awake. He blinked to clear some of the burn from his eyes. His lids felt like sandpaper.

A board creaked underneath someone's weight.

Someone was inside the house.

Chapter Thirteen

Jules felt the muscles in Toby's body tense, causing her internal alarms to sound off. She opened her eyes as he shifted away from her. Cold filled the space in between them as she searched his gaze.

He brought up his left index finger to touch his lips. She nodded, acknowledging his request for her to be quiet.

It was dark downstairs save for the light from the TV. The volume was turned down, but it was still set high enough to hear what was going on. One of the quarterbacks was complaining about how tough his job was mentally as he whined about the physical toll. After being in a chopper crash, she could sympathize with the aches and pains. Yet she wouldn't choose to go down that route every week as a career path. Being in football must be like experiencing a car crash on a weekly basis.

No wonder those athletes got paid the big bucks and most were forced to retire in their twenties or early thirties. The body could only take so much. This might be what they did for a living, but it was no way to live. Not for her, anyway.

Those random thoughts were her brain's way of distracting her from her fears based on the look on Toby's face. Something had set him off.

He located his weapon and then handed hers to her. More evidence something was about to go down.

She flipped off the TV with the remote, plunging them into darkness. One of the requirements when she'd put money down on the new-build town house was the ability to make it appear like nighttime at any given point in time in the home. Jules sometimes had to catch up on sleep after a case and needed darkness to be able to pull it off.

The blackout blinds were coming in handy now as she took the lead, heading toward the stairs.

A board creaked, causing her pulse to skyrocket. Someone was inside her home.

Footsteps followed a pattern of someone sprinting across the room. Did the intruder realize they were waiting?

"Stay here," Toby whispered as he stepped in front of her. He was doing his best to protect her, but that didn't fly.

"This is my home, Toby," she whispered back. "My home."

He moved aside without so much as a word so she could pass by. Toby, of all people, would understand the need to protect his own domain.

Pointing out that she was in a better position to nail a target considering she had the use of her right hand would only add insult to injury.

By the time she reached the top of the staircase, it was eerily quiet on the second level of her home. She knew every creaky board in her house, so she walked across the landing like she was in a game of hopscotch.

Stealthily, she moved to the guest room, where she'd heard the noises coming from. The lights were out upstairs too, but the sun came through the opened windows. Toby followed closely behind, keeping enough distance to be able to watch her steps and shadow her movements.

Weapon at the ready, leading the way, she entered her guest bedroom. Toby stepped in behind her, flipping on the light. With his back to hers in case the perp came up from behind, they moved through the room.

Jules checked inside the closet first, then underneath the bed. She moved to the window, which was ajar. "He either came in this way or used it to escape."

Having an intruder inside her home felt like the worst kind of violation. She closed and locked the window, for all the good it did because she never left town without making certain her house was like a vault.

Moving into her office next door, they performed the same routine. Then the primary bedroom was checked, followed by the bathroom. Once the home was clear, they checked the windows, searching for any signs of someone running away.

They saw no signs of anyone.

"It's all good in here," she said, sitting down on the edge of her bed. She noticed that her underwear drawer was slightly open. Again, that wasn't her doing.

She pushed up to standing and then cut across the room. "What is it, Jules?"

"Bastard stole my underwear," she said with an involuntary shiver.

WHITE-HOT RAGE burned Toby from the inside out. "So, this sicko can come after us, but we aren't supposed to go after him?"

"If it's him, he's taunting us," Jules said, always practical. He had no idea how she pulled off staying calm in a situation like this. "Think about it. Taking a US marshal down with him would be a pretty good high for a lowlife like Symes. He wants you to make a mistake and come after him so he can flip the script, sending you to jail."

"He couldn't have known I was here, Jules." Toby shook his head. "He was coming for you."

"I caught him staring at you a couple of times during transport," she admitted. "Didn't think too much of it at the time. But there was an intensity that was enough to catch my attention."

"Why didn't you say something?"

"For one, I had no idea about your sister or that he could possibly have been the one responsible," she said, throwing her hands up. "You don't think I would have withheld information like that from you, do you? If I'd known there could be a connection to you?"

He shook his head. "Of course not.".

"You didn't trust me enough to tell me about what happened to Lila or what's been going on since," Jules said.

"Trust had nothing to do with it," he countered. There was no way in hell he would allow her to believe that he didn't have full confidence in her. "I'm the one who's broken, Jules. I'm the one who brings devastation down onto everyone I care about."

Jules reclaimed her seat next to him on his left side and then set her weapon on the nightstand before taking his and doing the same. A mix of pity and sadness morphed her features.

"Don't feel sorry for me, Jules. That's the worst thing you could do. That look. The one on your face right now is half the reason I never spoke up about what happened. I didn't want you to look at me that way."

She turned to face him, bringing her hand up to his face. Her touch wasn't much more than a feather but sent rockets of desire firing through him.

As she moved closer, her gaze dropped to his lips. Toby's pulse kicked up several notches as heat flew south. Temptation to lean into her, into *his* Jules, was the strongest pull he'd ever experienced. Magnet to steel.

A rational voice in the back of his mind said he should stop this while he was able. Was he able, though? Because he'd never experienced anything that was anywhere near this powerful. He could only imagine what a kiss would be like if his body hummed with need being this close to her. Her fresh, clean, flowery scent overtook his senses. All he could think was...*more*. He wanted—no, needed—more. He needed to be close to Jules. He needed to breathe her in to remind himself that he was still alive. That life was still worth going through the motions for. Right now, he needed to feel her lips moving against his.

Toby leaned in, closing the distance between them as he pressed a tentative kiss to those sweet lips of hers. Would she pull back? Reject him?

He had no idea how this was going to go, except that the sound of her racing heart matched his. Those tender lips of hers were the sweetest taste. And nothing inside him could stop now that they'd touched.

A deep groan surfaced as he felt her tongue slick across his bottom lip. Desire like he'd never known filled him, tempted him to keep going when logic said their friendship could be on the line if they continued.

Friendship? His brain argued he'd never looked at Jules as a friend or he would have been able to handle hearing about her dating life.

Did she feel the same way about him?

Or was this pity?

The last thought gave him enough willpower to pull

back. He rested his forehead on hers as both tried to catch their breath.

"Was that a mistake?" he asked, searching for a sign she wanted this to happen because her feelings ran deep and wasn't just trying to comfort him out of pity.

"Not on my end," she said before putting more space between them. "But it can't happen again."

Toby had to clear the frog in his throat before he could speak. "Right."

"I can't lose you, Toby."

Even Jules seemed to realize he would mess it up between them, ruining any chance they could go back to being friends when he did the inevitable.

"Agreed" was all he could say.

She turned away from him and then picked up her 9 mm. "We need to call this in."

"I know," he said. "Let's get our supervisor on the phone."

"Think he'll be surprised you're at my house?" she asked.

Would that make Jules look bad? Because he didn't care about himself. "I doubt it. Mack is sharp. He knows we're close. I imagine that he would expect us to be together after what we've been through. And then there's the fact we can both use the company."

"True," she said.

"Plus, the investigator on the case needs to know we're being targeted by this creep," he continued as the being-in-love-with-his-best-friend fog lifted.

"I'll go downstairs and grab my phone." She started to get up, but he reached for her hand.

"Hey," he said. "Being with you, making love to you, would be the most incredible experience of my life." Saying the words out loud was easier than he'd expected it to be. "No one compares to you, Jules."

Her eyes twinkled with something that looked a whole lot like need, which wasn't making it any easier to step out of this moment. They had to, though. She was too important to risk losing her.

"We both know that's not an option," he continued. "And the real rub is that no one will *ever* compare to you."

She cocked her head to one side, deciding if she agreed. "And you still think it's a good idea to stay platonic?"

"It's not a choice, Jules."

She sat there for a long moment before tucking a stray piece of hair behind her ear. "Okay, then. Let's never talk about this again."

Damn.

Knowing she was spot-on didn't ease the sudden ache in his chest or the feeling of loss threatening to consume him like an out-of-control wildfire. At this point, he would welcome the burn because it would remind him that he was still alive.

Shutting down all feelings for Jules other than friendship meant numbing himself.

So be it.

"Let's head downstairs together," he said, standing up. Without those larger doses of pain medication, Toby felt everything. He noticed the dull ache in his right wrist. He knew when it broke there wasn't much they could do to repair the injury. Reduction, the doctor explained before surgery on his side to remove shrapnel, meant the doctor repositioned the bones to allow them to heal correctly. Then immobilization using a soft-sided cast prevented movement after realignment. All fancy terms for saying the doc straightened him out and now nature needed to do the work.

Not using his right wrist for anywhere from six to twelve weeks meant riding a desk when he was cleared to go back to work. Considering the investigation underway, he would most likely have to attend some type of mental health evaluation too. *Yippee-ki-yay.*

Toby could think of dozens of better ways to spend his time off from the job other than nursing a broken wrist and all the other injuries he'd acquired. Normally, those thoughts might include a leggy blonde. Not this time. And maybe not for a while. It wouldn't be fair to the other person when his heart wasn't into dating.

Then what?

Shoving those thoughts aside, Toby headed downstairs with Jules not far behind. She flipped on lights as they moved.

"I knew I should have replaced the windows here," Jules said once they reached the kitchen. "I did with the ground floor but naively assumed no one would go to the trouble of coming in through the second story."

"Most people don't even get that far," he said.

"We know better, Toby," she said. "I have no excuse."

"Except no one believes anything like this will happen to them," he pointed out, not ready to let her blame herself for something this perp did. "You did more than most by replacing them downstairs. Plus, you have an alarm for when you're away."

"We should have armed it," she said.

"Hell, I don't even lock my door half the time," he said. It was true. He lived on the outskirts of town, where no one was a stranger.

"The whole town where you live knows one another," she said. "Everyone watches out for each other."

Who watched out for Jules?

Chapter Fourteen

Once again, Symes had outsmarted Jules. He'd taken the key to his handcuffs off her, as well as her backup weapon. Now he'd broken into her house while she was home and stole a pair of underpants.

What the hell?

Rather than chew on that or beat herself up further, she set those thoughts aside long enough to make the call to her supervisor.

"I'll have someone staked outside your property to watch out in case he returns," Mack said after the circumstances were explained. Then came, "Do you think it would be best to head to Mesa Point now?"

"I can't leave Toby to fend for himself," she countered. "Not in his current condition."

"You're right," Mack conceded. "Can you take him with you? It might be a good idea for him to get some fresh country air. It can be good for healing."

"Neither of us are in any condition to make a drive," she said as the wheels in the back of her mind started churning. "As soon as we are, though, it's not a half-bad idea."

"I can send a car," Mack said. "Whatever you need. Just let me know, and I'll make it happen. You deserve protection."

"Much appreciated, sir," she said, thinking it might not be a bad idea to stay at the family paint ranch. "I'll discuss the idea with Toby and let you know what we decide."

A thought struck. Would she be bringing danger to her family's doorstep?

Then again, all six Remington grandkids had gone into the US Marshals Service. Would they be more protected in Mesa Point?

"That's all I'm asking," Mack stated, exacerbated. After perfunctory goodbyes, Jules ended the call and locked gazes with Toby. He was already shaking his head.

"You go," he said. "I'll head to my place."

Did he think Symes would leave her alone if they were apart?

"And then what?" she asked.

"You'll be with family, and I'll take care of myself while I heal," he said, point-blank.

"Why not come with me?"

"Because that would be like me admitting defeat," Toby said on a sharp sigh. "Allowing Symes to control where I go, when I go, is essentially handing over the reins. I can't do it."

"Then let me come home with you," she said. "I'll head to Mesa Point after."

"Do you really want to stay away from your family for days or weeks while I heal?" he countered.

"I don't want to be away from my siblings, cousins and grandparents, but you are just as much a part of my family to me as they are," she said.

"You have that determined look in your eyes, Jules. Don't dig your heels in on this subject. I'm not worth it."

"You are to me," she said.

"That's not helping." He put a hand up to stop her from

continuing down that path. Then he moved into the kitchen and started making coffee.

"I'll take a cup," she said, figuring there was no use fighting Toby once he'd made a decision. She sat at her kitchen island, seething at the fact Symes got away with something so personal of hers.

Taking underwear was a sign. He was telling them that he could break in and take whatever he wanted. The jerk must have come out of the crash in better shape than either one of them.

Had he followed them? Was he stalking her?

Or was Toby right? Was Symes using her to taunt Toby? Was he still out there somewhere? Lurking?

Eleven years.

Who could evade law enforcement for eleven years while actively raping and murdering? Most who got away didn't continue their activities. They disappeared, fleeing the US once they realized every law enforcement agency was looking for them. They reasoned it was only a matter of time before they were captured if they stayed in the US.

"We need to check into Symes's file," she finally said to Toby. When she looked up, she realized he was studying her while the second cup of coffee brewed. She had one of those pod machines that did all the work and was easy to load. Everything in Jules's life was built for ease, since she gave 110 percent of her energy to work. "How much do you know about him?"

"Not more than you," he said. "I didn't make the connection that he could be the one responsible for Lila's murder until you told me about the tattoo, so I had no reason to dig deeper into his file." Toby shook his head. "Absolutely not."

She pulled her best innocent-me act. "What?"

"First of all, you're supposed to be healing, not logging

on to your work files," he pointed out. "Second, there's a digital trail that could point the finger right back at you as the person helping me in this ridiculous chopper crash theory."

"But—"

"No," he warned. "Your computer activity will be watched and so will mine. No one keeps hard copies anymore. Everything is digital."

"There has to be news stories about him by now," she countered. "He's been big news ever since his arrest a week ago."

"True," Toby said as the machine spit and sputtered behind him, mimicking coffee-shop sounds. The stainless steel and sleek black model was meant to give her an experience, not just a cup of black coffee. It also made lattes, but she was more of a straight black coffee person. It helped her think more clearly. Right now, she could use a gallon.

"We need to learn everything we can about Symes," she said as her brain cells started firing again.

"Not from one of your devices," he shot back as he handed over the first mug, then waited for his to finish brewing.

"Because?"

"It will implicate you in helping me," he said.

"The man broke into my home, Toby. We reported it to Mack. I have every right to know who just violated my privacy and stole my underwear."

Toby didn't have a counterargument there.

"Plus, if we use someone else's device, it'll make us look guilty," she continued. "I deserve to know who I'm really dealing with in case he returns." The thought caused her to shiver involuntarily. She couldn't go there mentally with what the man may intend to do with her undergarment. That just creeped her out further. "And if this creep decides killing me is the ultimate snub to you, I want to know every possible weakness the man has."

It didn't take long for Toby to agree there. She was right. No one could argue.

"What do you want to do?" he asked, joining her at the marble island with his fresh brew.

"Let's do a search," she said, grabbing the nearby laptop. "You're right about not logging in to work. We can do some investigative work right here. No need to access those files when we have the internet."

"All right," Toby said after taking a sip of coffee. "Let's see what comes up."

The term *less is more* didn't apply to information on a serial rapist and kidnapper. There wasn't much more than a few basic details of Symes's arrest. He'd been caught leaving a crime scene, too late for the victim, with the cello string he'd strangled her with, along with a shoebox full of souvenirs from the crime.

"He keeps souvenirs," Toby said after reading the same passage. "We already knew that about Lila's killer, but this is more evidence linking Symes to my sister's death."

"How did he stay in the South and Southwest without ever being captured?" she asked. "His murders go back eleven years, and that's just the ones we know about. We don't know how many victims there were." *Hold on a sec.* She had a fingerprint kit. Could she dust her upstairs window from the outside?

Neither one of them was in shape to climb a ladder. The dresser might be easier to lift a print from.

"Keep reading," she stated. Though the man had never previously left a fingerprint at a crime scene, you never knew when a slipup might happen. Then again, adding breaking-and-entering charges along with petty theft wouldn't exactly add much time to rape and murder charges. The crime he'd committed today was peanuts compared to what he usually did.

Was she right about him biding his time? Targeting her?

Did he settle for stealing her undergarment when he realized she wasn't home alone? Had he intended to do much more to her? Or maybe the better question was, did he plan to rape and murder her?

Over my dead body.

Then again, he probably preferred it that way. She couldn't begin to think about Toby's sister's case. At eighteen, she'd been young and innocent. A baby in the grand scheme of life, despite feeling those first steps toward real independence.

Had Symes targeted her specifically because of her brother's job? It made sense when she thought about it as she retrieved her spare fingerprint kit from her garage, where she kept extra supplies. He would go after someone young and innocent. He would take pleasure in ripping her world apart, which made him one twisted individual.

No one had come forward to claim he was a brother, stepbrother, son or stepson in the articles she'd perused. Maybe Toby had found something when she'd left the room.

Then again, who would want to claim ties with a monster?

No former girlfriends gave interviews, as sometimes happened in high-profile cases.

Jules entered the house through the garage door leading into the kitchen.

"Hey," Toby said as he studied the screen. "I might have found a connection to Symes in Amarillo."

"That would give him easy access to Texas, New Mexico and Colorado," she said off the top of her head.

"Don't forget Kansas and Oklahoma," Toby quickly pointed out.

"Not to mention how easy it would be to cross the border to Mexico," she added.

"Someone, somewhere, has information about this bastard," Toby said. "My money is on figuring it out in Amarillo." He sized her up. "How soon before you'll be able to drive? Honestly."

"My personal vehicle is in the garage," she said, flexing the fingers on her free hand. "Seems like my hands work fine."

"Your knee, though," he said. "You're still in pain."

"There's not much I can do there," she responded.

"Except keep it elevated, which you wouldn't be doing while driving," he reasoned.

"Do you want to find this monster?" she asked, knowing full well Toby did. Would he do anything to catch him? Toby would draw the line if he thought an activity would hurt her. Other than that, she believed everything else might be on the table.

"You know that I do, Jules."

"So do I," she said. "He made this personal with me, Toby. This isn't just about you anymore."

"The investigators will say that we don't know for certain Symes was responsible for the break-in or missing underwear," he said, being reasonable. "They'll suggest we jumped to conclusions and might even ask how you can be certain your underwear is missing in the first place."

"You know how I operate," she said. "My drawers would pass the harshest military inspection. My underwear has been messed with and a pair is missing. I restocked after doing laundry before leaving for the trip." She felt her cheeks flame. "Plus, the sexier red silk pair is missing. It's my date pair." Not that she'd been on a whole lot of those recently.

Suddenly, the rim of Toby's coffee mug got real interesting. Was it the thought of her dating in general or specifically dating other men?

Their kiss, brief as it had been, had sizzled with the promise of the best kiss of her life if they hadn't stopped before the point of no return.

Toby had been clear about not wanting to go there and risk their friendship. She heard him loud and clear and was still embarrassed she'd actually considered asking him for more. Chalking her heightened emotions up to the heat of the moment, Jules needed to keep herself in check. Because it was a little too easy to imagine herself with Toby in the biblical sense. He didn't want that, and she didn't go where she wasn't welcome.

Getting a person to have sex with her had never really been a problem before, so she'd been mortified when Toby had pulled away.

It was good, though. This way, their friendship was still intact, and they would get to stay in each other's lives for the long haul.

And that was cool. Right?

"I can drive, Toby," she finally said. "Besides, we don't have another choice." She made a dramatic show of looking him up and down. "It's not like I'm letting you get behind the wheel."

"What about Mesa Point?" he asked after a chuckle that caused him to wince in pain. She felt bad about that part.

"I can't bring this monster home with me to Mesa Point," she said. "There's no telling who he will hurt to get to me. The hospital doesn't have enough security to ensure no one slips into my grandparents' room. How difficult would it be to pull a plug? Or tamper with a medicine drip? This needs to end with him being recaptured and then locked up for the rest of his life."

Toby sat there, contemplating.

There was no way she could do any of this without him. She would beg him to go with her, if that was what it took.

After what felt like an eternity, he said, "It's an eight-hour drive. Let's roll."

Chapter Fifteen

After roughly four hours on the road, Toby insisted Jules stop to take a break. She'd yawned four times in the last five minutes, a sure sign she needed rest. Amarillo could wait until morning. Getting in at night wouldn't do any good anyway. It was the kind of place where the streets were rolled up after dark. Knocking on someone's door after sundown without being expected could get them shot.

Most folks didn't lock their doors and didn't need to. Not with a shotgun within arm's reach and, possibly, a couple of dogs bred for protection that ran loose on the property.

After stopping off near Abilene for food and a bed to sleep in, they were back on the road by five sharp the next morning.

"Do you think he followed us?" Jules asked as they entered Amarillo, also known as the gateway to Palo Duro Canyon State Park and for its location in the Texas Panhandle. The flatland had just sustained serious wildfires that were finally contained, but they could have impacted the person they came to speak to—Jodie Symes Benning.

If Toby's research was correct, he'd dug up Symes's cousin. If his hunch was right, someone had been hiding Symes. To be fair, Jules had had the same idea. Considering they both had the same feeling, it was worth investigating.

Besides, all they could do at either of their houses was sit and wait. Mack would probably say sit and heal, but even their supervisor seemed frustrated by the turn of events.

Since they were on medical leave, they could go anywhere they wanted and do anything that suited them. Their story was that a road trip would do them good.

Could Symes have beaten them to the punch?

Toby doubted it. Mainly because they'd slipped out of town not long after the break-in. He might circle back once he deemed the coast was clear, but he wouldn't risk sticking around when the area would be watched by law enforcement agencies. In part, the protection was for Toby and Jules. The other, larger factor was that every law enforcement officer wanted credit for taking Symes off the street.

"He sent me a piece of Lila's hair on the first anniversary," Toby said as they turned down the road leading to Jodie's home. She lived out in the boonies on five acres of land. According to Google Maps, she had a small barn on her property that most likely housed a horse or two. Her own home was a modest ranch-style. Jodie was widowed and had no children. Though, she was written up as school bus driver of the year two years in a row by the district where she worked.

"That's awful, Toby," Jules said, breaking into his thoughts. "I can't imagine how awful that must have been for you."

"It was in a Ziploc baggie with the label *LW* on it." The memory of standing on his front porch as he opened his mail to see a lock of dark hair with his sister's initials on it hit full force. Suddenly, no pain in his body could come close to the emotional damage on that day.

Jules shook her head.

"I dropped it," he continued. "It just fell out of my hands, and the winds were so strong that day they picked it up. It floated a little bit before landing on my concrete porch."

Jules pulled off the road, but he barely noticed. "What did you do?"

"Tried to hold it together," he shared. "Which was the most difficult thing I've ever done because I was supposed to protect her."

"It wasn't your fault, Toby."

"Really? Because it sure as hell felt that way at the time," he snapped. He didn't mean to snap at Jules, and she seemed to understand when she reached over and touched his hand.

"I think you've been holding on to that guilt and blame for too long." She kept the engine idling, but the vehicle was in Park. "When none of it was your fault."

Toby nodded, but he couldn't let himself off the hook so easily. "I was all she had, and I told her to fight."

"That gave her a chance," Jules said gently. "It might have even worked. Or at the very least given law enforcement something to work with, like his DNA underneath her fingernails. It's the same advice any of us would have given."

"Yeah, but you didn't," he pointed out. "It was me. I did. And she suffered for it."

"So have you," she reminded him. "Except that you have to live with this for the rest of your life."

"I need this bastard behind bars," he said, feeling the emotions push their way to the surface, begging for revenge.

"That's why we're here," she said. "To get information and put him away for the rest of his life where he can't hurt anyone else."

Toby nodded. The all-too-familiar anger rising to the surface and battling for control. It would be so easy to let it take the wheel, especially now that Symes had targeted Jules. Was he trying to take everyone Toby loved away from him?

The short answer was probably yes.

Then it dawned on him. This was personal. "It just occurred to me that I must have come into contact with Symes at some point in my life. Except I don't remember that name at all." He paused. "Shouldn't it ring a bell?"

"You think Lila was targeted because of you?" Jules asked. "Because I was under the impression that maybe this guy got extra pleasure out of finding out she was related to a US marshal."

"I didn't recognize him," Toby said. "Wouldn't I?"

"Not necessarily," she said. "You didn't remember me from the coffee shop."

"I'm still questioning that one," Toby admitted.

"Exactly," she stated.

Toby searched his memories and came up blank. He would have remembered Jules if he'd seen her. But she knew who he'd been with, and he couldn't deny Dark Roast was one of his favorite Austin coffee shops. He'd most definitely been there with the brunette Jules had mentioned seeing. The proof was there. And yet it was still difficult for him to see it.

What else was he missing?

"Did Lila date anyone that you knew of?" Jules asked as she navigated back onto the dusty road. Most folks outside of Texas thought major cities like Dallas, Houston and Austin still had tumbleweeds rolling around and that everyone rode horses to the grocery. Amarillo was the place that might actually happen. It was almost infamous in the state for its blistering wind and horrific ice storms.

"No," he said.

"No one she told you about or she didn't date at all?" she continued.

"Both," he said with confidence that was now shaky as they pulled in front of Jodie's property.

"The main thing I know from being a sister with two brothers is that I certainly didn't tell the boys everything," she said. "I'd be far more likely to tell my female cousins personal stuff like who I was interested in or hooking up with when I was younger."

Despite being friends, Toby wanted the subject of Jules's hookups to be off-limits. Was that wrong? He must have winced, because she popped him in the arm.

"What? You don't think guys were interested in me when I was eighteen?" she asked.

"Not the problem," he informed her. "I'm certain too many guys wanted to get to know you."

"I didn't, by the way," she said. "Hook up with strangers or guys on campus. I was too busy studying and trying to stay in school to date a whole lot."

He doubted it but appreciated the effort to spare him the details.

"What?" she asked, catching on. "You don't believe me?"

"Someone like you would have guys knocking on your door constantly," he said.

"I'm pretty sure that I didn't give off the vibe that any advances would be welcome," she countered. "Dating in college wasn't big on my list."

Good. Despite the fact it was none of his business, he was relieved she didn't date around. Part of him didn't want to share her with anyone else.

Jules pulled into the driveway of the redbrick ranch. The house looked smaller compared to the oversize lot. The gravel driveway contrasted against the yellow landscape where weeds choked out every sign of greenery.

Survival of the fittest.

JULES PARKED HER four-door sedan. "I've always wanted a convertible."

"Why not buy one?" Toby asked, clearly confused by the change in topic.

"Because I live in San Antonio, not Galveston," she stated, figuring she needed to get him out of his dark mood before they talked to Jodie. Prodding him back into investigation mode might help them better assess the person they were about to interview. Plus, his thoughts had taken him to a dark place. One she wasn't altogether certain she could drag him out of.

Toby needed to maintain sharp focus. He was one of the best marshals she'd ever worked with, and she didn't want him to lose sight of that fact, because he was clearly still beating himself up for his sister's death—a death he had no control over, no matter how much he believed that he could have somehow changed the outcome.

No one got to change the past. If Jules could, she would go back and drive her grandparents home the night they suffered a near-fatal crash. The people who'd taken her in and raised her didn't deserve to be fighting for their lives right now.

Life could be hella unfair.

Jerks seemed to live forever when lovely people suffered a horrific fate. No one knew which door they were going to get. She'd decided it was up to her to make the best of her life a long time ago.

But she hated realizing how much Toby blamed himself

for his sister's murder. She hated how hard on himself he was. And that he couldn't let go of the guilt.

Could she?

The problem was that she blamed herself for her grand-parents' crash. She blamed herself for not being there for them as they got older. She should have anticipated something like this happening and wasn't ready to let herself off the hook.

Except reality was dawning on her too. No one got to control what happened in life, least of all her or Toby.

Life had its own deal. It was their job to navigate it and somehow survive when a real awful hand was dealt to them.

Thankfully, they had each other to lean on. At least, when Toby let her in. Because more than anything, she wanted to take some of the burden from his shoulders. She wanted to ease some of his pain, but that meant he would have to open up.

Was that even possible?

She parked next to the redbrick home with green shutters. There were a couple of pots on the porch with dead branches sticking out of dry soil.

Toby exited the vehicle first and then came around to her door. Despite his dominant hand being in a sling, he opened the door for her. She didn't mind. It was ingrained in him to be polite, a gentleman, and she appreciated the gesture.

"Before we talk to Jodie, I just want you to know that you can talk to me about your sister anytime," she said. "I'd like to know more about her. What she liked to do in her free time and the kinds of books she liked to read." Mostly, Jules wanted to know more about the person instead of the statistic Lila became.

"I'd like that," Toby said, surprising her. He reached for her hand and squeezed. And then he locked gazes with her.

For a few seconds, she could see all the bottled-up hurt that he'd locked away for the past five years since his sister's death. "What would I do without you, Jules?"

The way her name rolled off his tongue, that deep timbre that was so good at breaking down her walls, caused this moment between them to feel like one of the most intimate of her life.

But she couldn't keep walking down a path to nowhere. She pulled her hand back and gave his arm a light tap. "Let's hope you never have to find out, buddy." Her attempt at a smile was weak at best. *Buddy?*

Wow, Jules, you're really bringing home the friendship point, aren't you? Great job!

Toby's laugh was awkward at best. But, hey, there was no use tricking herself into believing that they could be more. She'd been tempted. He'd been clear about where he stood. Continuing to flirt with the idea they were perfect for each other would just be punishment at this point.

Jules exited the sedan. She'd changed into black slacks and a cotton pullover shirt. For a second, she debated grabbing her shoulder holster out of the trunk. Would it put Jodie on guard if they showed up looking official? Technically, they were on medical leave, and this was an informal visit. Curiosity about Theodore Symes brought them to the area.

This was dancing very close to a line that couldn't be crossed. As citizens, however, and as a victim of a breaking and entering along with burglary, Jules had a right to know more about Theodore the Terrible.

"Who should do the talking?" she asked, realizing they hadn't discussed strategy on the drive here.

"Do you want to take the lead?" he asked, clearing his throat.

Was he afraid his emotions would get the best of him?

It wasn't like Toby to be unprofessional, but this situation was unique.

"Yes," she agreed.

Before they reached the first step on the concrete porch, the door swung open and smacked against the wall. A woman in curlers and a dress robe stepped out as she brought a shotgun up, aiming the business end directly at them.

"If I were the two of you, I'd turn around and get off my property before I shoot," the woman who had to be Jodie Symes Benning stated.

Chapter Sixteen

Toby brought his good hand up in the surrender position, palm out. "Hold on there, ma'am. My friend and I want to ask a couple of questions. That's all. We aren't here to cause any trouble."

Jodie lowered the barrel and sized them up.

"Maybe we come inside?" Toby asked in the tone that was so good at getting him what he wanted from women in the office. "We just want to talk."

"Are you a reporter?" Jodie asked. She was average height with the body shape of an apple. Everything about her was practical and simple, from her brown house slippers to her rose-covered dress robe. At least, he thought that was what the zip-up covering was called. It fell well past her knees, revealing not much more than her ankles. She looked older than her forty-two years, which put her a decade older than both him and Jules.

Make no mistake about it. The woman seemed as tough as the landscape where she lived. On this early November morning, a cold front brewed. Crisp wind cut through his joggers.

He must look a mess when he really thought about it, showing up unannounced with his arm in a sling and bruises on his face and body. Jodie couldn't see the bandage where he'd taken a piece of metal underneath his ribs on the right side. Between the pair of them, they looked like they'd just come back from war.

"No, ma'am," he said, pulling on his Southern drawl. Most folks couldn't tell he was from Texas unless he needed to break out the accent to build rapport. In his experience, folks were comforted by someone they could relate to. Someone they felt like they could run into at the quickie mart or big-box store while running errands. "Rest assured, we aren't anything of the sort." He twisted his face in disgust to drive home the point.

"Then who are you and why are you on my property?" Jodie asked, suspicion keeping her eyebrow raised as she studied them.

"Two people looking for answers," he said before introducing himself. "This is my friend Julie."

Jules took a step forward and stuck out her hand. Jodie eyed the offering but didn't budge.

"What's your business with me?" Jodie pressed, unyielding. The fact she didn't immediately kick them off her property or shoot was reassuring. She'd also lowered the barrel and curled her arm around the shotgun in a relaxed position.

"We came to ask if you'd seen or heard from Theodore recently," he said. The ranch house could be a good hiding place. Jodie was a cousin, so there wouldn't be a whole lot of suspicion there unless it was revealed the two were close.

What motive would she have to hide Theodore? Putting her neck on the line to save her cousin without cause didn't ring true.

She tilted her head and shot a look that said Toby might be delusional. "No."

"When was the last time you spoke to him, if I may ask?" Toby continued.

"Four years next month," she stated without hesitation.

"The two of you were close at one time?" Toby asked, realizing there'd been a connection in the past at least. Had she figured out what a monster the man was? Banned him from visiting? From her life? Had she been hounded by reporters who figured out the connection between the two?

"Yes," she said, twisting her face.

Jules seemed to catch on to something Toby missed. She clasped her hands together, staving off the chill in the air. "Did you have some kind of disagreement or falling-out with Theodore?"

"Why would I?" Jodie asked, with more questions stamped in the creases in her forehead.

"So, you two were close at one time," Jules continued, unfazed.

"Two peas in a pod," Jodie said. "Right up until his death."

Whoa. Toby didn't see that one coming.

Jules must have pieced it together. She didn't hesitate in offering condolences. "I'm sorry for your loss, ma'am."

"Teddy was a good man," Jodie said.

"May I ask how he died?" Jules continued as Toby managed to pull out his phone. He'd never been all that great with his left hand. His current condition was giving him an opportunity to work on that.

He managed to pull up a picture of Theodore the Terrible.

"Black ice after a storm blew through," Jodie supplied with a face made of stone. "His truck sank into a pond when he went off the road, and he was pinned by his seat belt." She might see showing emotion as a weakness.

Had Toby done the same all these years? Or kept his feelings bottled up because he feared they might break him if released?

"That's awful," Jules said with so much compassion Jodie's chin quivered.

"Well, nothing can be done about it now," Jodie continued, straightening up broad shoulders.

"True," Jules agreed. "Still, it must be hard with the holidays coming up."

Jodie gave a slight nod.

"Would you mind if I showed you a picture of the man we're trying to locate?" Toby asked.

"Go ahead," Jodie said, taking a step forward as Toby did the same. He extended his arm out as far as possible so as not to make the woman feel threatened in any way. Not that he could do much damage in his current condition. Stretching out his arm hurt like hell.

Jodie shook her head. "Never seen that man before in my life."

"He has the same name as your cousin," Toby said.

"That must be what those reporters wanted to jabber about," Jodie said, shaking her head. Someone who lived out on a property alone didn't appreciate folks showing up unannounced. They also didn't trust the government in most cases.

"You didn't talk to them?" Jules asked.

Jodie's forehead creased again. "Why would I? Ain't done nothing wrong. My cousin's been gone four years. Figured there wasn't any good that could come out of those people being here." Her face twisted like she'd just sucked on a pickled prune.

"I can't stand reporters any more than you," Jules agreed.

In their job, news leaks could damage a case. In some instances, reporters could be useful. In his experience, they did more harm than good until a criminal was caught. Then they were good at getting information out quickly and accurately. The problem with news in recent years was speed turned out to be more important than accuracy in too many cases. Putting information on the internet from a law enforcement agency directly proved more useful.

Jodie's shoulders relaxed. "Never had much use for 'em."

"Is it possible your cousin knew the man in the picture?" Toby asked, shifting the conversation back to Symes.

"Anything is possible, I guess," Jodie said with a shrug. "My cousin was always taking in strays. He fixed up a shed on his property that he kept unlocked for folks heading through town that got caught by a storm or needed to bed down for the night."

"How did people find out they could stay there?" Jules asked.

"All anyone had to do was ask," Jodie supplied. "Everyone knew about Teddy's open-door policy."

"Everyone?" Jules echoed.

"That's right," Jodie confirmed. "Bernie at the gas station would send folks to Teddy all the time."

"Your cousin sounded like an amazing person," Jules said.

"He was," Jodie agreed. "Anyone who needed a meal just showed up at his back door at 6:00 a.m. sharp. He pinned a note next to the coffee machine for people who stayed over. The place out back was outfitted with a commode and shower but not much in the way of a kitchen."

What were the chances the two men randomly shared the same name? An idea was taking shape in Toby's mind. He needed to discuss it with Jules when they were alone.

"THANK YOU FOR taking the time to talk to us," Jules said as information swirled in the back of her mind.

"It was no trouble," Jodie said. "Stop by anytime."

The woman was being polite. She surely didn't want to be disturbed again.

"I have a couple more questions," Jules said. "If you don't mind."

Jodie nodded. "Go ahead."

"Did you ever stop by in the mornings and see any of the men who stayed over at Teddy's place?" Jules asked.

"Not really," she said. "No." There was no hesitation in any of her answers, which most likely meant she was telling the truth. That was one of many signs, including body language cues, that when put together helped an investigator determine the honesty of answers. "I'm sure I was there a couple of times over the years when someone showed up at the back door, though."

"Did you remember seeing anyone with tattoos?" Jules asked, digging for any hint the woman might have seen Symes—or whoever he really was—without realizing it.

"I've seen a few," she admitted. "In my cousin's house, cowboy hats could stay on, so most just hung their heads and ate, not wanting to disturb Teddy if he had company."

"Any of the grim reaper underneath a brunette?" Jules asked. It might be a long shot, but it was worth trying.

Jodie's gaze flew up and to the left, a sign of attempting to recall information. "Can't say that I did, but then, I don't remember anyone without sleeves on."

Of course, Symes would hide his tattoos from anyone who could identify him by those marks.

"We appreciate it," Toby said with his usual charm. He was probably the reason Jodie didn't come out shooting. One look at Toby disarmed women of all shapes and sizes. The whole square-jawed, model look broke down a lot of barriers.

He touched her elbow, causing a firestorm in her body

on contact. The warmth helped deal with the cold air on the way back to the sedan. Temps were dropping by the minute.

"Have you checked the weather lately?" she asked after settling into the driver's seat.

Toby palmed his cell after clicking on his seat belt, then studied the screen. "Looks like a front is headed this way."

"Think we should get out of here before it hits?" she asked.

"We got what we came for," he confirmed. "What do you say we head back?"

"My house or yours?" she asked, not really wanting to go back to hers after the break-in. It had been too easy for Symes.

"What do you think about heading to Austin instead?" he asked, surprising her with the idea. "We could stay downtown. Use cash if we stop by an ATM."

"I know a good coffee shop," she stated with a smile as she started the engine and then backed down the driveway.

Once they were back on the road, Toby redirected the small talk. "Are you thinking what I'm thinking?"

"The reason Symes has been slipping through everyone's fingers is because he's stealing people's identities?"

"Yes," he said. "That way, he hides in plain sight."

"No one is looking for 'Teddy' Symes," she added. "But whoever he was last might be in question."

"I've been thinking we might be overlooking something important," he said.

"Like he has to have had some kind of training or experience that allows him to survive under all types of conditions and circumstances," she stated.

"Exactly," he agreed.

"Survivalist? Doomsday prepper?"

"Could be one of those," he said. "Or something more formal."

"Military training?" she asked. "Because I was afraid of that one."

Some doomsday preppers could be just as militant, living off the grid and placing themselves in extreme conditions to test their readiness for what they deemed the end of time. Others prepped out of fear and wanted to be ready to survive if the world as they knew it collapsed or there was another world war.

But former military who crossed a dark line could be the deadliest.

Still, something had to trigger a person to turn into a monster like Theodore the Terrible. Jodie would despise what the man had done to her cousin's name if their hunch turned out to be true. All signs pointed to it being the reality of what had happened.

Jules's first instinct was that Symes murdered Teddy in order to take his identity. Or he might have learned of the man's death and, much like a vulture, took advantage of the situation after it presented itself. Who knew how many other identities Symes had adopted over the past eleven years.

"Why Amarillo?" she finally asked, thinking they might need to turn around to find out Symes's connection to the location.

"He might have been passing through and needed a place to sleep for the night," Toby explained. "That could be how he originally found out about Teddy's place. Who knows how many years he's been using it. He could slip in and out without anyone ever knowing he was there."

"Makes sense," she said. "Wouldn't he have had to change

his appearance enough to slip under the radar of wanted posters?"

"Folks mind their own business in places like Amarillo," he said. "Plus, the town rolls up the streets at dusk. He would have understood these kinds of details."

"True," she agreed. "And they would be so used to folks coming and going from Teddy's place they probably wouldn't even notice anymore."

"Symes is smart enough to figure out that he could slip through town under the radar with a network in place like Teddy's."

"He survived without being captured for eleven years for a reason," she agreed. "Which makes me think he had a reason to be in places like Amarillo before he started killing."

"Truck driver comes to mind," Toby said. "Is it too easy?"

"Not really," she said. "Not for this kind of criminal activity. Truck drivers moved through states with deliveries throughout the Southwest."

"There'd be records," he said.

"He might have worked under an assumed name then too," she said.

"If we're going to make any progress in this case, we're going to need his real identity," Toby reasoned.

"How do we go about that?" she asked, stumped. If they had a town or city name and approximate age, they could peruse school records. Yearbooks were a useful resource once some information was known about a person's identity.

"Good question," Toby said.

Jules glanced over and realized he had an idea. "Am I still driving toward Austin?"

He pulled up his phone.

"Give me a sec" was all he said as he studied the screen. Why did Jules think she was about to bang a U-turn?

Gray clouds filled the sky. She checked the thermometer gauge on the dashboard. The temperature had dropped ten degrees since she'd last checked.

"If we don't leave now, we could end up trapped in bad weather," she said to Toby a few seconds too late.

He had that look in his eyes.

Could they get what they needed and get out before the storm?

Chapter Seventeen

"We need to stick around and ask more questions," Toby said. He had an idea, but he wasn't sure Jules would go for it.

"I don't like the sound of your voice right now, Toby."

"We need to try," he said. "We can ask at a gas station if the new owner of Teddy's home kept his tradition alive. At the very least, we need to poke around and see if Symes, or whoever the hell he really is, hid anything inside a mattress or floorboard." He heard his tempo rise alongside his excitement level. "Think about it. He's probably stashing evidence somewhere along his trail. It would be too risky to keep it on him."

"We don't know for certain he stayed at Teddy's," she countered, but there wasn't a whole lot of enthusiasm in her protest. In fact, based on the way she was tapping her thumb on the steering wheel, she was coming around.

"Have I ever told you what a great driver you are?" Toby hedged, attempting to use his charm on her.

"Compliments won't get you very far with me," she said, dryly. "You should know that by now." She tapped her thumb a little faster. "Plus, you know that I learned to drive in Texas."

"Meaning?"

"I have no idea how to drive on icy roads," she said with a shiver. Did she recall black ice was the reason Teddy had died?

"I'd never ask you to," he said reassuringly. "You mean too much to me for that nonsense."

"Like I said, buttering me up will get you nowhere, Toby Ward."

"A guy can try," he shot back, thankful she still had a sense of humor, based on her tone.

Her stomach growled.

"How about we stop for food first," he said, realizing they hadn't eaten for hours. It was past lunchtime, and Jules wasn't the kind of person who could skip a meal.

"I can't remember the last time I've eaten at Whataburger," she said, motioning toward the orange-and-white sign past the next red light.

"Let's do it," he said, thinking he could go for one of their signature double meat burgers and fries about now.

Jules turned into the parking lot and then entered the drive-through line. "Okay if we eat inside the car? I'm not in the mood to be stared at."

"I'm good with it," he said. "We can watch traffic if you park toward the street."

"Sounds like a plan to me," she said, pulling around to the menu board.

Ordering took all of two seconds. There wasn't much of a line, so they were parked out front and eating in a matter of minutes.

Jules leaned her head back on the headrest, a small moan of pleasure escaping from her lips—lips that were none of his business. "I was hungry."

"I know."

"I feel much better," she said.

"I know."

"I should keep a protein bar in my purse at all times to avoid times like these," she said.

"I know."

The problem was that he did know her a little too well.

Ten minutes later, they were headed toward Teddy's small ranch that was off County Road 21, where there was a whole lot of dry ground. Tinder?

At least the weather front would douse what was left of the wildfires, especially if sleet came through like the weather app on his phone predicted.

"How much time do we have before it hits?" Jules asked. "The temperature dropped another twelve degrees since we stopped for lunch."

He studied the weather app. "You know how predictable Texas weather can be."

"You're avoiding the answer," she said. "Give it to me straight."

"I'd plan on staying the night here in Amarillo," he stated.

"Hell's bells," she said under her breath. The words she wanted to use were probably a whole lot stronger. "Then let's get some answers while we're here."

The biggest downside to being trapped in a town was the obvious fact they couldn't leave. Then there was the reality they might be here for a few days, depending on this front. Neither had packed an overnight bag. "We should probably swing by the store and pick up supplies for the night."

"As in camping?" she asked with a whole lot of concern in her voice.

"I was thinking more along the lines of clothes and food," he said.

"It's probably better to prepare for the worst-case scenario," she reasoned. "This isn't the kind of place you want to be caught off guard in during a storm."

She was right except for the goodwill of ranch owners. He suspected there were others who kept an open door for folks moving through. Seasonal workers, ranch hands and the like would need a place to bed down for the night while heading to their next job. Growing up outside of San Antonio, he was familiar with stories like these despite never having used one himself.

Jules pulled into the nearest big-box store. The convenience couldn't be beat. Being able to buy pretty much everything they might need in one stop made life easier.

"How many days are we shopping for?" Jules asked after parking.

"Let's go with three, just to be safe," he said.

Taking in a sharp breath and then releasing it slowly, she said, "Okay, then. Let's get to it."

"Let's roll."

JULES AND TOBY must look like quite a pair, considering how many folks performed double takes as they gathered supplies. Did they look as battle weary as she felt? She couldn't imagine the amount of pain Toby was in, considering he'd had a small piece of metal removed from his right side. His pain tolerance must be out of this world, because he refused to take medication on schedule, stating that his injury amounted to a scratch and he'd be fine. She suspected he wanted a clear mind.

Watching as he walked, she realized just how much pain he must be in.

"Should you take something stronger than ibuprofen?" she whispered as they neared the checkout with their cart full of clothing and easy-to-eat food. The chip and water

aisles had been ransacked ahead of the storm, which made
her smile. Some things stayed the same no matter where
she was. Apparently, folks could do without a lot of things,
but potato chips wasn't one of them.

"I need to stay sharp," he reasoned.

"What if you need to run?"

"Then I'm going to have to hope adrenaline kicks in," he
admitted as he stacked items onto the conveyor belt while
the cashier rang up the person in front of them.

"That's a risky move," she said.

"You have 'supplies' in your trunk?" he asked, referring
to weapons.

"Yes, I do," she said.

"That should help." He grabbed more items, wincing as
he moved. Both of them needed rest in order to heal.

The thought of Symes out there, able to continue his
twisted activities, was the only fuel keeping her going at
this point. Plus, he'd made this personal when he stole from
her. The item he'd taken was surely meant to send a message to both Jules and Toby that he could take what he
wanted right under their noses.

Jules involuntarily shivered.

As disturbing as it was, Toby was right. They needed to
think like Symes in order to anticipate his next move. Recapture him or lead law enforcement to him—either way,
the result would be the same.

Tapping her credit card on the payment terminal, she then
helped place the bags inside the cart. Toby was stubborn
enough to want to pull his weight, so she wouldn't argue.
By the time they made it back to the sedan and placed the
bags on the back seat, his skin was pale.

They would have to take a break once they got to Teddy's
old place.

Toby leaned his head back on the headrest.

"Why don't you close your eyes on the ride to the ranch?" Jules urged.

"I tried on the drive here this morning," he said. His voice took the quiet tone it normally did before he shut down on her. "All I could think about was the memento the sicko sent the second year."

Jules navigated onto the roadway, her grip tightening on the steering wheel as she listened.

"A sterling silver *L*," he reminisced. "It was tarnished, cheap. One of those prizes you win at the state fair. I'd thrown a football and let her pick the prize when she turned thirteen." He issued a sharp sigh. "She didn't go anywhere without it from that day on. Said it was her good-luck charm."

"I'm so sorry, Toby."

"I know." His voice was the kind of quiet calm that came before a massive storm.

"It wasn't your fault," she said.

He didn't respond. When he did, he finally said, "Year three was a piece of her shirt."

"The man, if he can be called that, is twisted," she said.

"Year four was fibers from the rope he strangled her with when he was done, except he didn't kill her," he continued. "He didn't realize she didn't die right then."

Jules took in a deep breath and slowly released it. "What about year five? What did he send?"

"This year?" Toby began. "A piece of cotton from the underpants she had on while he took her life."

"There are no words," she said to him. Offering quiet reassurances fell short but was the best she could do. Nothing could bring his sister back or take away the pain of losing her. Not to mention the fact he'd blamed himself all these years. Breathing must hurt under the weight of his guilt.

"There's nothing I can say to take away your pain. Just know that I'm here for you." Had Symes taken Jules's underwear as a reminder to Toby the man thought he could take whatever he wanted right out from underneath Toby's nose? "Was the last item he sent the reason you blame yourself for the break-in at my house?" Toby had taken it hard. Rightfully so, considering they were downstairs the whole time.

"Would you see it any other way if the tables were turned?"

"I guess not," she admitted with a better understanding of Toby's reactions to everything that had been happening.

"He's coming after me," he said. "Using anyone close to me to torment me."

"Once again, I have to wonder why," she said. "Why you? You're a good person. You wouldn't hurt anyone on purpose. This more than likely has to do with your line of work more than anything else."

Law enforcement workers were targeted at times for locking away a loved one or someone who was connected to a crime organization. It might be rare, but that didn't mean it never happened. There was a reason penalties went up for a perp harming a law enforcement official. The harsher sentences deterred criminals in most cases.

"I'm sure you already searched for anyone who might have a bone to pick with you," she said. "Someone you arrested who seemed particularly bent on revenge."

"The felons we track down, transport and put away generally have nothing to lose," Toby pointed out. "The list of felons who threatened retribution is long."

"The FBI would have tracked down that angle," she surmised. "Unless, of course, they missed someone." Again, a rarity.

Wind kicked up, blowing against the sedan so hard it

shook. She checked the temperature gauge in the console. It read a chilly twenty-seven degrees as the first shimmer of drizzle coated the front of her car. She'd taken note of the barbed-wire fence surrounding the property, the open gate and the home with a light on in what was probably the kitchen area.

Changing the subject, she asked, "Do you think we should knock on the homeowner's door?"

Toby shook his head. "If they mind us taking shelter, I imagine they'll come tell us. It's best to look like we know what we're doing rather than let them know we don't. You saw the way Jodie and the others at the store looked at us."

"Guess we stick out like sore thumbs with all these injuries," she said with a half smile.

"I thought it was my good looks," he quipped. The joke was meant to lighten the mood, even though he couldn't rally a lighter tone.

"Obviously," she reassured him with an eye roll. It was true, though. There'd been plenty of women in the store with their tongues practically wagging as he walked past. The fact he was impervious to it made him even more charming. But she'd spent enough time focused on his good qualities.

No one was perfect. She should probably remind herself Toby wasn't either. Her traitorous heart would argue the fact.

She parked behind the oversize shed. Wind bit through her shirt the second she opened the car door.

The wood structure might be old, but it appeared solid. It looked to be ten feet by twelve feet with cedar wood and a metal roof. The door was unlocked, as expected. Jules bolted inside to stave off the cold.

"Is there electricity?" she asked as she took in the space.

A set of bunk beds flanked each wall. Each had pillows and blankets, a luxury for a weary traveler. There was a kerosene stovetop on the back wall, along with a coffee maker attached to an electrical cord that ran down the back wall and out a small hole that had been sealed with caulk. She didn't want to think about the small critters it kept out.

"I don't think there's much more than what's plugged into the electrical strip on the back wall," Toby surmised after stepping into the middle of the room and turning a complete circle.

"Is that a space heater?" She didn't wait for a response. Instead, she walked to the back wall and pulled out something that looked like a radiator. Bending down to plug it in caused her to groan.

"Let me do that," Toby said.

"My knee is in better shape than most of your body parts right now," she quipped with a smile.

"Fair point," he conceded.

Turning on the heater gave instant satisfaction. "It works. Oh, bless."

Toby smiled at the Southern remark. "Kerosene lamps should help get us through the night."

"The storm is getting worse," she said, moving to the window. Cold seeped in through the small frame. At least they had a heater and were out of the wind. "It's already getting dark."

"I'll grab our supplies," he said. "We should probably be thinking about bedding down here for the night."

The idea of sleeping where a serial rapist and killer once laid his head gave her the creeps. But driving in the storm in search of shelter was the worst of bad ideas. They'd made it here. The place might be dusty, and it was clear men stayed here, based on the minimalism and half inch of dust no one seemed to bother cleaning.

"You need help," she said, following Toby to the car.

They brought in a few bags of supplies in two trips. She checked the small bathroom complete with a shower she could barely turn around in. The toilet needed to be soaked in bleach. A plastic tub of wipes sat on the back of the commode, along with several rolls of toilet paper.

Surprisingly, there were clean towels folded on the small vanity. The sink was recently used. Someone had been here.

Was it Symes?

Another shudder rocked her at the thought. Because another possibility was that he could be on his way here right now.

Chapter Eighteen

It took the last of Toby's strength to set up shop for the night in the makeshift bunkhouse. Jules managed to keep pace with him and wipe down the bathroom with the bleach wipes she'd found.

There was dust on the wood floors and pretty much everywhere else. But the place wasn't filthy. Someone cared about it, took care of it.

Teddy must have had a kind heart to make a place like this on his land for travelers. The black coffee and pot would be a godsend to most who needed to get up early and get on the road.

Scavengers like Symes turned Toby's stomach. He searched his memory to see if he could come up with any link between the two of them. His face didn't ring any bells, but they were older now. Years changed folks. Symes was supposedly forty-two, a solid decade older than Toby. At least, that was the lie. It was anyone's guess what the man's real age might be, which meant they could be similar in age.

Toby kept drawing a blank.

The other option was Symes had no idea who Toby was until after he'd killed Lila. Then the bastard, who kept me-mentos from every kill, decided to taunt a US marshal as a way to increase his high and possibly draw out the enjoyment. *Enjoyment* was a bitter word in conjunction with rape and murder.

"We should be set for the night," Jules said, breaking into his thoughts as he moved around on the floor, checking for loose boards. "Why not take a break and rest?"

He glanced at her, not ready to stop.

She put her hands up in the surrender position. "It's just a suggestion. This place isn't big. Any evidence hidden here shouldn't be too difficult to find considering we're trained professionals." She sat down in front of him. "You've lost coloring on me again. I'm worried about you."

Who could argue with her compassion?

Toby scooted until his back rested against the nearest bunk bed. "I can't help but think a sweet person like Teddy didn't deserve to have a monster taking advantage of his kindness."

"Do you want water?" she asked.

Toby nodded. Even he couldn't ignore the pain for much longer. And his body was weak. He'd been lightheaded after bringing in the supplies.

"Here you go," Jules said after reaching for a bag and grabbing a bottle.

"Thanks," he said, taking the offering. One too many times, he found his gaze wandering down to her lips.

Toby cleared his throat and then took a drink of water.

"Creepy to think he might have slept here, isn't it?" she asked, taking a bottle for herself and opening it.

He nodded.

"I doubt I'll be able to sleep," she said.

"If we can doze on and off, that'll be better than nothing," he agreed. This close, he couldn't stop thinking about taking the bastard down.

"Did we make a mistake in coming here?" She bit down on a plump lip.

"I don't regret our choices," he said. "What else would we be doing, anyway? The man is hunting us. Otherwise, he never would have risked tracking us to your place."

She shivered.

"Do you think he'll keep coming after us until he's re-captured or finishes the job he started at the chopper?" she asked.

Toby shrugged. "I wish I knew. It's probably good that I don't think like him. Right?"

"Guess I never thought about it like that," she admitted. "It's true, though." She issued a sharp sigh. "I keep thinking about Captain Crawford."

"Same here."

"It's awful," she said. "What if he is someone's husband?"

"I noticed a gold band," he said.

"I did too," she admitted. "And then I kept thinking he might be someone's father. Now a kid or kids will have to grow up without him."

A gust of wind shook the structure. Jules gasped before bringing a hand up to cover her mouth.

They were both jumpy and for good reason. Under normal circumstances, Toby wouldn't doubt the two of them going up against one person. But now they were injured, barely operating. They needed rest.

Another gust threatened to shatter the window. Jules's eyes widened.

"Hey, come sit next to me," he said, holding up his good arm.

She moved over to him and curled up in the crook. "I was afraid of my own shadow when I was little."

"How did you get over it?"

"There was this one day when I distinctly remember deciding nothing got to scare me again," she said. "I think my fears stemmed from being abandoned or something. I remember waking up in the middle of the night screaming until Grandma Lacy came running." She didn't lift her gaze to meet his when she spoke. Instead, she drew circles on the floor with her finger. "She would stay with me until 'the monsters' went away. I'm told I was little when I started having the nightmares. I'm not sure the exact age, but I was terrified of waking up and everyone just disappearing. Like in *The Wizard of Oz* when Dorothy is caught in the tornado. She had that little dog, Toto, and nothing else familiar. I was a hundred percent certain that I would wake up one day and everyone would be gone from my life."

"Must have been terrifying for a kid," he said, holding her a little tighter.

"It was," she admitted in a rare moment of vulnerability. In times like these, with her, all his protective instincts sprang to life. "And then, one day, I decided that I was never going to be scared of anything again."

"Were you?"

"Surprisingly, no," she said. "I mean, we all have our moments, right? But I've never experienced anything quite like those nightmares since." She paused. "Until now."

"Because of him?"

She shook her head, confusing him.

"Because I'm afraid of losing you," she admitted. Those words cut him to the core.

"You'll never lose me, Jules. I give you my word."

"It's not a promise either of us can make," she countered. "No matter how much we might care about each other and want to."

"There are never any guarantees in life," he said after

a thoughtful pause. She was right. "But as long as I have breath in my lungs, I'll be here for you."

"What about the future, Toby? What if we do survive this twisted individual? What then? We end up in relationships with other people? Our friendship slowly dies on the vine? I almost think that would be worse." She yawned. Jules always lost her filter when she was dead tired.

Toby regretted thinking of the word *dead* in conjunction with his best friend.

The point she made couldn't be argued. He had no plans to get married, but she was a beautiful, intelligent person who would end up married eventually. Her husband wouldn't want her best friend to be a guy. Toby could admit that he would be possessive over her too, selfishly wanting to be the only man in her life aside from her other family members.

Was it right of him? No. Probably not.

Emotions weren't rational. They took on a mind of their own. Wanted things they weren't supposed to have. Where was logic in times like these?

JULES HADN'T INTENDED to go down that road with Toby tonight. The day had taken on a life of its own. They were stuck inside a small shelter in what was predicted to be a once-in-a-decade storm, and a very twisted person wanted them both dead. *Dead* wasn't the right word. He wanted to torture Toby by—what?—raping and killing Jules. Meanwhile, the two other people she loved most in the world were in a hospital in Mesa Point, where she should probably be. Except she didn't want to bring a murderer to their doorstep.

After talking to her boss and putting a text in the family group chat, everyone was on high alert. Or, at least, they should be.

Her normal filter had taken a vacation, and she had no idea what was up from down any longer. She would, however, apprehend and contain Symes should he show his face here.

Would he get to them first?

That was the burning question. Toby was operating at probably 40 percent at best. She wasn't exactly as strong and rested as she could be. They'd survived a chopper crash.

It occurred to her that she was unsettled about something that might not even be reality. The creepy feeling she'd had since entering this space might not be warranted.

There was one way to find out. "Maybe we should investigate this space a little more. Figure out if Symes stashed anything here. It might help settle my nerves."

"Okay," Toby said. His deep timbre had a low, husky quality. The word *sexy* came to mind.

Shaking the thought loose from her head, she said, "It might be easier for you to take the floors, and I'll take counters and ceilings."

She half expected an argument, but Toby nodded instead. He seemed to realize that he needed to take it easy, which was good. Normally, he would keep pushing himself until he dropped.

Teddy never locked the door to the shelter, but maybe they could place a chair or some kind of barrier to let them know if someone tried to enter. If Symes tracked them to her house, how difficult would it be for him to locate them here?

Not very.

Would the storm slow him down? Or would it give him time to search them out? Find them? Finish the job?

A headache formed at the spot right between her eyes. At least the shelter was warm with the space heater. Otherwise, she was certain they would freeze to death. Nature would do the job Symes couldn't.

Shoving those thoughts to the back of her mind so she could focus, she ran her hand along the counters and then walls.

"I found something," Toby said.

She joined him in a heartbeat as he sat on the floor next to a bunk bed, a plank in his hand. Taking a seat next to him, she tried to ignore the thumping in her head. The plank had been two feet underneath the bed, so he had to reach into unknown territory to dig around.

"What can I use?" he asked, realizing he could put his own fingerprints all over evidence if they found something.

"We can use the flashlight app on my phone to see inside the hole," she offered. "Can you get on your stomach and slide under the bed?"

He shook his head with a look of defeat.

"I can do it," she said. Having the use of both of her arms made the difference in being able to pull herself underneath the bed. Icy fingers of fear gripped her spine at what she might find in the hole.

Jules braced herself as she handed Toby her phone. He locked gazes with her for a few seconds as though willing her to have the strength to keep going. Because who knew what other types of souvenirs Symes kept.

A blast of wind caused the electricity to stutter. Her heart rate jacked up several notches as she lay flat on her stomach and tucked her head down low to fit into the space. Was she about to be face-to-face with unimaginable horrors?

When Jules was a little kid, she hated eating turnips. When they were on the dinner menu, she closed her eyes tight, held her nose and went for it. The faster she got it over with, the quicker she could move on to the food on her plate she wanted to eat.

This was no different.

Toby stretched out his good arm, illuminating the space.

Jules couldn't close her eyes, so she took in a deep breath and then held it before scooting underneath the bed frame as fast as she could to get this over with.

The hole was at least a foot and a half deep. There was a banged-up metal box inside that was almost a perfect fit.

A cold shiver raced down Jules's spine.

"There's a box in here, Toby," she stated after releasing her breath. "But I need to find a way to get it out without putting my fingerprints all over it."

For a split second, the light went out and Toby disappeared. He returned a few seconds later to a clap of thunder that shook the floor.

"Here's a fork," he said, handing it over as he lit the area underneath the bed again. "Will that work?"

"Let's give it a try," she stated. Using the fork as leverage underneath the metal handle, she lifted the box. It was the size of a small tackle box. This felt a lot like that game called Operation, where you had to pluck a fake body part out of the man with the red Rudolph nose. Make a mistake and the buzzer would sound. In this case, make a mistake and she could erase key evidence.

"Steady," Toby said. His calm, smooth voice washed over her and through her, giving her the confidence she needed to successfully lift the box out of its tomb.

Something dawned on Jules. *Spiders.*

She was able to bring the box out from underneath the bed frame and set it on the floor without dropping it, which was a miracle in its own right.

"The owner of this box was here recently and probably visits often," she said.

Toby cocked his head to one side. His left eyebrow arched. "How do you know?"

"There are no spiderwebs in the hole."

Chapter Nineteen

Toby sat up, staring at the metal box in front of him. The metal clasps reminded him of old school lunch boxes. His pulse raced. His heartbeat thundered in his ears, smothering out all else.

"How can we open this?" she asked, and he could barely hear her over the noise in his head, despite her being right next to him.

"Let me try," he said, glancing up at her and locking eyes for a split second. That was all it took to ground him again. Jules had that effect on him. No matter how far gone he was, she always brought him back. Funny thing about it was that she never even realized it had happened or that she was responsible for bringing him back to the light.

Jules handed over the fork. He finagled it until the metal clasp opened. Then it was a matter of sticking the utensil into the handle to lift the lid.

"Here we go," he said as it opened. Split down the middle, the box revealed its contents as the lid hit the wood floor with a clank.

Jules covered her mouth as a gasp escaped. "It's here. We have proof the monster has been here."

There was an assortment of items in Ziploc bags with initials on them.

Toby sat back before bringing his left hand up to rake through his hair. He wiped down his face, realizing his chin had a couple of days' worth of stubble. It was strange what the mind noticed when faced with something so horrific.

Normally, his job was to track down felons after a warrant had been issued. Presently, he was on prisoner rotation, which was glorified babysitting while felons were transported. Until it wasn't, which was how he'd found himself in this current predicament.

Predicament was too nice a word. He was living a nightmare fueled by one twisted individual.

"Maybe these items will tell us more about him," Jules offered. "Help us locate him."

He's coming for us. Toby held his tongue. Jules knew it too. It was the reason her words held no confidence. They both realized this perp had set his sights on them. Would Symes pull back?

Using the fork, Toby shoved baggies around like unwanted peas on a plate. "There has to be something here to help identify who Symes really is."

The corner of something that looked a whole lot like a photograph could be seen at the bottom of the box.

Toby managed to shove the Ziplocs around enough to get a good look at what it was. There were two boys in swimming suits. One looked to be a teenager, roughly fourteen or fifteen years old. He had his arm around a younger boy who looked to be around eight or nine. The younger boy smiled wide, revealing a few missing teeth.

"It's him," Jules said on another gasp. "It's Symes."

Toby managed to flip the picture over with some finesse. The back read: *Reed and me.*

"The older boy looks familiar too," Toby said. It was then he noticed the folded-up newspaper article.

"What?" Jules immediately asked. "Toby? What is it?"

"I know Symes's real identity," he stated, feeling the blood drain from his face. Because he was guilty. No excuses. This was his fault. And that was how he knew this man wouldn't stop until Toby paid the ultimate price. But first, he intended to torment Toby and show him loss. "His brother drowned on my shift as a lifeguard years ago."

"How did it happen?" Jules asked.

"I saw him pick a fight with a smaller kid, pushing him under the surface of the water in the deep end, laughing," Toby explained. "I blew my whistle, thinking I was high and mighty, but the teen blew me off."

"Understandable," she said. "I'm sure you followed your training."

"I did," he agreed. "However, by the time I got in the water, the smaller kid was in serious trouble, so I went to him first without realizing the teen was being run over by a rowdy bunch on a blow-up canoe." He shook his head. "There was something in the air that day. It seemed like all the kids were restless, looking for trouble. We had a group of older teens. I'm guessing this guy thought he would look cool by picking on someone."

"Teens do weird things sometimes to fit in," Jules pointed out.

"All I could think about was protecting the smaller guy," he said. "I didn't even look back to see if the tormentor was all right."

"You couldn't have known what was happening," she said. "And there had to have been other lifeguards there that day."

"Jackson called in," Toby recalled. "Said he was sick, but we all knew his girlfriend was throwing a party at her parents' lake house. We were short-staffed."

"And a teenager yourself," she was quick to remind him. But he didn't think that acquitted him. He'd been hired to do a job, which was keep swimmers safe in the water. No matter how much of a jerk the teen was being, it was Toby's responsibility to look out for him.

"My ego got in the way, and I turned my back on him," Toby said.

"And you've been carrying around the guilt ever since," Jules said quietly, almost reverently.

What else should he do? Saving lives was his responsibility.

"You do realize that you couldn't have known what was happening behind your back or that the teen would drown," she reminded him, reaching out to touch his arm. There was something special about the way she touched him. Like she always reached his soul with her lightest contact.

"Doesn't release me from my responsibility," he countered.

"I understand," she said. "Do you blame me for…what's his real name?"

"Axel Holmes," he supplied. "His brother Reed went by the nickname Champ."

"That's unusual," she said.

"According to the article—" he motioned toward the worn, yellowed piece of folded paper at the bottom of the box "—his father had named him based on what he wanted people to shout from the stands."

"A sports fanatic?"

"To the nth degree," Toby said. "The article said Champ had a promising football career. To me, he was just a bully in the pool."

"Someone who is athletic can usually take care of themselves," she added, trying her best to give him an out he had no intention of taking.

Jules caught his gaze and locked on. Determination caused her to bite down hard before she spoke. "Do you think I'm responsible for Axel's escape?"

"No."

"Do you blame me for the man breaking into my home and stealing my underwear?" she pressed like a defense attorney in court on a roll.

"Of course not, Jules," he quickly countered. The last person she should blame was herself. It took a second, but it dawned on him what she was trying to do. Rather than put up an argument, he shook his head and cracked a small smile. "I hear you."

"Then you have to let yourself off the hook too," she said. Before he could respond, she added, "And if you can't do that today, promise me that you'll go easier on yourself moving forward."

"Have you ever considered going to law school?" he asked.

His question clearly caught her off guard. Her face wrinkled.

"What does that have to do with—"

It was her turn to catch on.

She tapped his arm. "I'll look into it if you'll consider forgiving yourself."

He could add negotiator to her long list of good traits. Jules was one of a kind. But she was right earlier. They wouldn't be able to stay this close forever. Someone, at some point, would get in between them.

The thought nearly knocked his breath out. Could he do anything about it, though?

JULES WOULDN'T PRESS the issue. Not when Toby was seriously considering her point of view. He didn't put up a counterargument, which was a good sign. New ideas worked in the back of Toby's mind until he made a decision whether or not to accept them. More often than not, he came to see reason.

She would let her comments marinate and hope he could find some leeway in his heart for past mistakes—mistakes anyone could have made. Most would move on without a second thought. That was what made Toby so special. He cared. Deeply. Even when he didn't want to admit it.

He was also too hard on himself, demanding things he would never expect from another human being.

Toby's gaze fixed on a certain Ziploc with the initials *LW* on it. He managed to scoot it against the metal wall and then out of the container. Her heart hurt for him as he studied the contents: a ring, a piece of cotton from what looked like her pajamas, an ankle bracelet and eyelashes.

Those were the only remnants left in the baggie of his sister. The evidence storage system suggested the crimes were well thought out. The lack of DNA evidence left behind that could be traced to him meant Axel was thorough. That was to be expected from someone who'd evaded capture for eleven years.

Now they knew that he slipped in and out of other people's identities too. In the mix were Social Security cards and copies of driver's licenses, along with birth certificates. She had no idea on sight how many were legal copies or doctored. Axel held a genuine hatred in his heart for women. Rape suggested he felt inferior. What trauma in his life caused him to want to take out his rage on innocent women? His victims ranged in age from late teens to early thirties. None looked the same, so it was women in general the man hated. Blamed?

"I can't believe he would blame you for his brother's drowning after all this time," she said, mainly thinking out loud.

"He was eight or nine years old when it happened," he recalled. "Look at the way he's looking up at his big brother like he's some kind of hero."

"One person's bully can be another person's saint, I guess," she considered.

"Depending on the circumstances, yes," he stated. "There was a case that ended with me talking to a mother whose son had committed horrific crimes. She covered for him. Hid him. Refused to admit she'd even seen him around until the FBI threatened to arrest her nineteen-year-old daughter for prostitution if the woman didn't reveal where she was hiding her son."

Jules had had similar cases.

"Rather than give up her only daughter, she gave us the location of her son," Toby continued. "I was on the arrest team. We had to bring the mother in a van to point out her son's identity because he'd gotten one of his friends to box him, hitting his face until it was almost unrecognizable. The man could sit at a table next to law enforcement at a restaurant and not be identified."

She nodded.

"The mother ran out of the van, wrapped her arms around her son's knees while he was handcuffed and begged his forgiveness," Toby revealed. "Her son had killed the woman's new husband because he said the man looked at him wrong. Still, the mother believed the son was a saint."

"Hard to believe," she said, shaking her head.

"He'd been paying her rent for two years, ever since his

father's death, had bought her a Mercedes to drive around in and fancy clothes," he explained. "She believed he was the best son that a mother could have."

"Even evil lives in shades of gray," she admitted.

"I could have been a real twerp, but my sister would have thought I hung the moon," he said. "Would she ever be able to forgive a person who was responsible for my death?"

"You didn't hold the boy's head underwater," she felt the need to point out, even though she understood his point.

"To Axel, that's exactly what I did," Toby said.

"It doesn't excuse what he's doing," Jules stated. Talking about family made her realize she should touch base with hers. She palmed her cell phone and checked the screen. "Off topic, but do you have any bars?"

Toby checked, then shook his head. "Sure don't."

"I guess I should have expected as much out here in the middle of a sleet storm." Sleet pinging the metal roof sounded like they were taking live rounds.

An apology crossed Toby's features.

"It was my idea to come out here, remember?" She felt the need to point it out so he didn't add this to his list of reasons to blame himself.

"I know," he said. "But I should have done a better job of protecting you."

"You already are, Toby," she said. "I just wish you could see it too." Then she added, "Plus, we protect each other. It's what partners do. You have my back, and I have yours. Remember?"

Toby didn't answer. His slight nod said she'd gotten through what could be a thick skull when he wanted it to be.

Figuring it was best to let Toby sit in his thoughts, she got her own fork and then went back to the Ziplocs. There were twenty-three. Twenty-three lives cut short. Twenty-three families left devastated. Twenty-three women who would never grow old.

Moments like this put life into perspective.

As much as she didn't want her grandparents to leave this earth, they'd lived long, full lives filled with everything people were meant to experience. There'd been hardships, good times, surprises and setbacks. But most of all, their lives had been filled with love. They were quick to forgive and first to encourage.

They lived beautiful lives filled with work they wanted to do and people who loved them with their whole hearts.

Maybe they had it all figured out after all.

Still, as long as there was fight left in them, she would beg them to stay, wishing for at least one more hug, family dinner and holiday season with them.

Looking down at these Ziplocs brought home the fact that even the longest of lives was still short.

Why waste a second of it?

A gust of wind cut into her thoughts, causing her to jump practically out of her skin as debris slammed into the exterior wall.

"Toby," she said, reaching for him as she tried to breathe.

"I'm here," came the reassurance, quick as lightning to a dark room.

She hoped her sedan would be okay out there without being parked in a garage. It was their only mode of transportation. The second the storm let up and the roads were safe, she wanted to get out of here.

They were in Axel's territory now.

Chapter Twenty

Jules shivered, even though it was warm in the shelter thanks to the heater.

"Wish we could figure out how bad this thing is predicted to get," she said, rubbing her arms as though to warm them.

Toby regretted her being involved. He wished one thing in his life could remain untouched, free from his curse. "We could always go to the main house and ask. The new owner is most likely stocked with better equipment, possibly a satellite for emergencies. The person would also likely have a generator in case power goes out, which I imagine happens a little too often around here."

Winds howled at this point. The noisy metal roof that sounded like bullets striking did little to calm his raging headache. His side ached. And he was long overdue to take a pain pill.

The problem with medicine was that it dulled his senses too much.

"With the phones out of range, we can't call any of this evidence in," Jules pointed out. Her forehead creased like it did when she was in serious contemplation. "We can't ask if there's been any progress in the investigation."

"I doubt we'd get an honest answer there," he stated. Not

when they were considered suspects. Now that he understood his connection to Axel, Toby's thoughts circled back to Captain Crawford. "Do you think the captain was involved?"

Jules shrugged. "I've been wondering the same thing lately. At first, I didn't want to consider the possibility, to be completely honest. I'd never flown with him before, but he came across as a good guy."

"I had the same impression," Toby stated.

The heater flickered on and off. Jules cursed under her breath.

"There's enough kerosene in the lamps to get us through the night if the heat holds," he reassured her.

As frustrating as it was to get this far and have Mother Nature stop them cold, he wouldn't risk going back out. Not even to find a spot where he was in range to use his cell phone.

Could they trouble the homeowner to use an emergency satellite phone? If they were certain the new owner had one, it would be a no-brainer.

Toby pushed up to standing and moved to the window. There were no lights on at the main house. Was anyone home?

There was nothing more than a small barn on the property. Toby hadn't seen horses in the fields or a structure large enough to run a full-on horse operation. Which could mean the owner wasn't even around with no livestock to tend to.

He wished he'd asked Jodie a few questions about who'd bought her cousin's home and whether she knew the person well enough to see if he could ask them a few questions.

Then again, they hadn't planned on sticking around town. The plan had been to get Jules safely away from the incoming storm. It had been Toby's idea to circle back and check the shed. This was on him. He sat back down, frustrated with himself.

"Hey." Jules's voice broke through his heavy thoughts. "What are you thinking?"

He shook his head.

"You look worried," she continued. "Is it the storm?"

"In part," he admitted. That was as far as he was willing to go.

"We can barricade the windows to keep debris from flying through them," she started. "And we can block the door with…" She glanced around the room. "The dining chair." There was a small square table pushed up against the corner of the back wall that had two wooden chairs tucked in. She hopped up and went to work, securing the door by wedging the back of one of the chairs under the knob. "There. That'll keep us from being surprised."

She stood in the center of the room, glancing around.

"We don't need all of the blankets, so we can use them to insulate the windows," she said. "Thankfully, there are only two to cover."

Before he could get to his feet, she'd fixed blankets to cover the windows. It was smart because it would also keep glass contained in the event a window was hit with debris hard enough to break it. There was a reason weather people advised against standing next to a window during a storm. Being hit and killed by debris or broken glass took more folks out than anything else in a storm. Texas's version of Mother Nature knew how to throw one serious temper tantrum too. She had no qualms about tossing cars around or upending fifty-year-old oak trees to send them flying through home windows.

"You're amazing, Jules. Do you know that?" He couldn't

help himself from saying those words out loud. They were words she deserved to hear.

Jules shot him a glare that shocked him.

"What?" he asked. "It's not a crime to tell your best friend what she should hear every day."

"That's not the problem, and you know it."

She studied him. Hard.

"Then what?" he asked. She needed to tell him because he honestly had no idea why she would be upset with him after he complimented her.

Jules brought her hand up to her hip, where she fisted it. "You better not be saying goodbye to me, Toby Ward."

Was he?

JULES KNEW TOBY well enough to realize he would do anything in his power to protect her, including draw Axel away from her. "You better not plan to slip out of here when I go to sleep."

"I would never do that to you," Toby stated with enough conviction for her to believe him.

"Let me decide what's best for me," she said. "Promise you won't make a decision on my behalf without letting me weigh in."

He cracked a smile.

"Promise," she urged.

"You have my word," he finally agreed. Toby's word was better than gold bars in the bank. Gold prices fluctuated based on the market. Toby was unchanging.

"Okay, then," she said, realizing just how drained she was. The dull ache in between her eyes felt like a tiny person with a jackhammer working the inside of her skull. "I'm tired and I want to know that if I take a nap, you'll be here when I wake up."

He gave himself a once-over. "Where am I going to go in this condition?"

This time, she smiled despite the hammering hell going on inside her brain. "You make a good point there."

"Besides, leaving you alone would put you at greater risk," he reasoned. "Because he'll go after you either way. If we're together, we have a better chance at fighting this bastard."

"You've thought this through," she said.

"I have to because you're too important to me to lose," he explained, like it was as plain as the nose on her face.

The sentiment went both ways.

"Let's freshen up and try to get some rest," she said. "Maybe by the time we wake up, the storm will have passed."

Toby nodded. "You go first."

Jules figured she might as well shower while she had the chance. She piled her hair on top of her head and made quick work of washing off. She changed into the fleece joggers they'd bought at the store and then brushed her teeth.

Rejoining Toby, she asked, "Do you need help with a shower?"

"Is that an invitation?" he quipped, clearly proud of his comeback.

"Funny," she said, shaking her head now that the pain had lightened up somewhat. Showers had a way of washing off the day and hitting the reset button. "Do you think we should put the evidence box in the trunk before we get too comfortable?" It dawned on her they should do their best to preserve it. They had a name now and evidence. Axel would have a much more difficult time hiding. "While I'm thinking about it, I might as well send a text to my family and Mack."

Toby cocked an eyebrow.

"When we get cell coverage, the messages will go through," she said. "That way, I won't have to keep checking my phone."

"We should definitely tell Mack our current location, what we found and the reason we're here in the first place," he said, catching on to her logic with a proud smile.

Toby being proud of her shouldn't warm her heart in the way that it did. What could she say? The man had an effect on her like no other, and she'd learned not to fight it a long time ago.

He attempted to stand up on his own, immediately landed on his backside—a backside that wasn't awful on the eyes. "About that offer of help with a shower. Does it happen to start with helping me up?"

"I might be able to arrange a little assistance," she said, needing a few lighter moments to recharge her battery after the heaviness of finding and opening the metal box.

"And, yes, we should put the evidence in a safer place just in case," he said, a little more solemn now. "For safe-keeping."

"I can do that," she offered after helping him to his feet. "Why don't you strip as much as possible while I run it out to the trunk?"

"I'd rather keep watch behind you if you don't mind," he said, reminding her of the ever-present threat.

Jules nodded. "Let's see. How should I carry the box?"

Fingerprints were a tricky beast. Whether or not a good print could be lifted was affected by multiple conditions. For one, they had to remain intact to be worth anything. Evaporation could impact the quality of the print. Other things, like sunlight, temperature and humidity, could change what could be lifted and speed up the evaporation process. As a material evaporated, it lost volume, and if it shrank too much, fingerprint dust lost the ability to detect a print at all. Rough surfaces were notorious for making dust unreliable. Dried paint was the opposite. The smooth surface would make the print easier to lift. There were other ways to lift prints—using light, for example—but that was above Jules's pay grade. There was a reason agencies employed forensic specialists; DNA evidence wasn't as cut-and-dried as TV shows would have the public believe.

This box could be tricky considering it was tucked into a floorboard in a room that was cold, humid, hot and every other condition the weather concocted on a given day. This part of Texas experienced all seasons. Sometimes in the same day.

"Closing the lid is easier than clasping the lock shut," he reasoned as he studied the box.

"I can wrap it in a dish towel," she offered. "We might lose some prints externally, but this surface and these conditions might have already done that job."

"I agree," he said. "Let's close the lid first." He did so using one of the forks. That part was easy enough. Closing the clasp was going to be harder. Was it necessary?

"Let me see if I can find a paper bag in the kitchen," she said, moving in the direction of the small space. There were a couple of cabinets with minimal supplies in them. She located a carton of Ziploc bags, decided not to touch those. There was a hot plate, so maybe she could find something better to use than her hands.

She opened a drawer by the hot plate and, voilà, located a pair of tongs. "We should have checked the drawer sooner." She turned around with the tongs in hand.

"Yes, we should have," he agreed with a smile. "But what a find."

"I think we should take the carton of Ziploc bags from the cabinet," she said.

"Definitely," Toby stated. "Are they the same as the kind we found in the box?"

"I believe so," she said. As far as evidence went, they'd hit the jackpot here. Amarillo was a centralized location, which would make it easier for Axel to move through neighboring states as well as Texas. So much clicked into place with this find. Everything but the one lingering issue of Captain Crawford. If he was guilty of working with Axel, the pilot had paid the ultimate price. Among the artifacts found here so far, money wasn't one of them. It was the only thing she could think of in terms of swaying Crawford to mess up comms. "We need a list of names of anyone who had access to the chopper before we took off."

"I'm sure investigators will chase names down," he said. "And I'm also certain we're the last people they'd share them with."

"You have a good point there," she said. "Now that we're under scrutiny and on medical leave, all of our access will be cut off."

"True," he said. "But we wouldn't be naive enough to tap into work computers. If Mack gets the list, we have a shot at him sharing the names. Or at the very least, giving us a heads-up that it was confirmed foul play with regards to the chopper."

"Not sure how much good any of the information will do when I really think about it," she reasoned. "What we have here is so much more powerful. Crawford didn't survive the crash, so it isn't like we can go to him for information or squeeze him if he's dirty."

"It would be good to know what we're dealing with," he said. "And if anyone higher up is involved in aiding Axel."

"You make any enemies lately that I should know about, Toby?" she half teased. She removed the Ziploc carton with tongs, using a small plastic trash bag to collect more items with a smooth surface and a better chance at providing a good print. The more ammunition she had to connect Axel to the crime, the better. If he actually used the Ziplocs here, they were a good find. They'd prove he came to this place in case no fingerprints could be lifted from the metal box or evidence inside. In fact, it linked him to the evidence box. He'd been meticulous with his crime scenes. No prints had ever been lifted, and he'd never left behind DNA.

Then again, he'd been caught once. He'd led investigators to several crime scenes, proud of his work.

And now he was coming for her best friend.

Chapter Twenty-One

After gathering evidence, Toby moved to the bathroom and managed to shimmy out of his pants. Those dropped to the floor with ease compared to trying to take off his shirt.

"All right," he said into the crack. The door was ajar in case he needed help. He hadn't been ready to admit defeat until now. "I give. I'm tapping out. I need you."

"Thought you'd be calling me," Jules said as she opened the door.

"You must have been standing right outside," he said.

"Figured it would save time when you needed me," she supplied. "Why don't you sit down on the toilet lid, so I can help you off with your shirt."

He'd managed to get out of the sling okay. Taking off a sweatshirt was a whole other ball game. That had to come over his head. He struggled to pull his bad arm inside, figuring it was a good first step to pulling the sweatshirt over his head.

"Here, let me help with that," Jules said.

He ignored the way her beautiful eyes glittered every time they were this close, focusing instead on something that wouldn't cause all blood to fly south and him to tent his boxers. An oil change. The pickup he used to tool around on his property needed an oil change.

Yep, that did it. Blocking out all thoughts of Jules and focusing on something mundane did the trick as she helped him remove his arm from the sleeve and then tugged on the left sleeve to make it easier for him to repeat that on his working side.

After that, it was her job to slide the sweatshirt over his head.

"Remind me to wear button-ups or zip-ups from now on," he said as he raked a hand through his wild hair.

"We might have only bought pullovers," she said with that characteristic sneaky smile that had ways of burrowing deep inside his chest.

"Sounds about right," he said with a chuckle that was worth the pain. "I might need a little more help than I realized."

"Okay," she said, the nervous edge to her voice threatening to unravel his resolve. "What can I do?"

"Stay close, just in case," he said.

"Will do," she said. "I can hold up a towel if you'd like to finish getting undressed."

"Sounds good," he said, holding off on standing up and stepping out of his boxers until she gave the green light. It came a couple of seconds later.

Then his boxers were on the floor. He would have to be careful not to get wet the bandage underneath his ribs where the doc had removed a small piece of metal. His body didn't seem to realize how small the piece had been, because it hurt like hell. The last thing he wanted to do was rip out twelve stitches, so he was careful not to raise his arm too high as he stepped into the shower stall and turned on the water.

The cold hit him fast and hard, but it also reminded him that he was alive.

The water took a second to warm up. By the time it did, his entire body was like ice.

But when warm water sluiced over him, he felt halfway decent for the first time today.

He kept the shower short and sweet. As he turned the spigot off, Jules stuck a towel inside the stall.

"Here you go," she said. "Do you need help drying off?"

"I should be good from here on out," he reassured her. "Thanks for being here, though. And for everything else you've done for me over the last few days. Hell, years, if we're being honest. I'm still trying to figure out why you chose to sit down next to me on your first day."

"Because you were the smartest person in the room," she said.

"You couldn't have known that," he countered.

"True," she said, "so I had to go with the best-looking guy in the room instead. I just told you that you were smart to pump up your ego."

He could hear the smile in her voice—that same damn smile that burrowed a little deeper this time.

"Jules, you never told me that you had a crush on me," he quipped.

Another crack of thunder boomed, shaking the structure that was protecting them from the elements.

It reminded Toby to hurry and get dressed.

Working faster meant more pain. To hell with it. No choice.

With heroic effort, Toby managed boxers, joggers and socks. Next came a T-shirt.

"Found a zipper hoodie," Jules said with a hint of pride in her voice. "Turns out we weren't completely oblivious to how difficult getting clothes on and off would be for you."

He accepted help in shrugging into the hoodie and then

moved out of the small space that felt a little too intimate. They'd moved the evidence to a safer location. Jules had texted their supervisor with the latest information. She'd updated her family so they wouldn't worry. They'd gone over the shed a couple of times to make sure there was no other evidence hiding in the walls, cabinets or flooring.

"Think you can get a little rest?" he asked. There wasn't much left to do while they waited out the storm.

"I can try," she said.

Toby already realized closing his eyes would be a bad idea. Seeing the Ziploc with his sister's initials had sent him into an emotional tailspin. One that had been working in the back of his mind no matter how much he was trying to force it out.

Close his eyes and those horrific images from the crime scene would haunt him.

"Keep me warm?" Jules asked, a catch in her voice as she motioned toward the bottom bunk farthest away from a window.

"Of course," he said, hearing the low, gravelly quality to his own. What could he say? Jules had an effect on him. She would always have an effect on him. He'd learned to live with it because they weren't always this together. Distance kept him from going for something that he could regret later.

Would he, though? Because he was beginning to think it was far worse not to step up to the plate than to bat and miss.

Toby shook off the sentiment as an effect of him being bone-tired. His thoughts took on a life of their own when he was exhausted. And *exhaustion* wasn't nearly big enough a word for what he felt.

Jules took his left hand in hers and led him to the bed. "You want in first?"

"No, you" was all he managed to say.

She climbed into the den-like space and then scooted all the way back to the wall. The twin-size bed wasn't nearly large enough for him to spread out. Before joining her, he retrieved both of their weapons.

After tucking their guns under the mattress, he maneuvered himself underneath the covers. Her warm body pressed firmly against his as she curled herself around his left side. On his back, Toby positioned himself so that she could settle into the crook of his arm.

Being like this with Jules made the world right itself in Toby's eyes.

Within a matter of minutes, her steady, even breathing indicated she'd fallen asleep. A growing piece of him liked how safe she must feel in his arms in order to surrender to sleep. He closed his eyes and, surprisingly, drifted off too.

JULES WOKE WITH a start. She immediately sat up and banged her head on the top bunk. Toby reacted to her movement. Gun in hand, he was up and out of bed in a heartbeat.

"What is it?" he asked. "What did you hear?"

She looked around, trying to orient herself. "Wind?"

Toby sat on the edge of the bed and then rested his elbows on his thighs as he leaned forward. "What time is it?"

There was no clock in the shed, nothing that would require electricity beyond what the strip was capable of producing and nothing that required babysitting with battery replacement. Folks passing through here brought their own time with them.

She checked her phone. At least the clock function still worked. "Three."

Toby rocked his head, still on high alert.

"Did you sleep at all?" she asked, scooting beside him after stretching out her arms.

"A little," he said.

"You woke me up twice, snoring," she teased. It was true, though, and she hadn't wanted to wake him.

"Guess I got more than a little, then," he said with a laugh that caused him to wince.

Seeing him in this level of pain made her question their decision to be so far away from home. "How do you feel?"

"I've been better," he quipped with a devastating little half smile. The show of clean, white, straight teeth was enough to cause the ladies in the office to talk at a higher pitch. She'd be lying if she said he had no effect on her.

"Same here," she admitted. "Coffee? I think I can figure out how to make some."

"Might as well go for it," he said. "Who knows how much longer we'll have electricity."

He barely got out the words when the power went out.

"I think you just jinxed us, Toby."

"Sorry about that," he said with too serious a tone for her offhanded comment. It reminded her just how much he blamed himself for everything that went wrong.

She wanted to point out that he should give himself more credit. Focus more on everything he did right, which was a lot. Since her words would likely fall on deaf ears, she held her tongue. For now. When the right moment struck, he was going to get an earful. He should know just how wonderful he was, how many lives he'd saved and how important he was to everyone around him, including her.

"We should check on the main house," he said, cutting into her thoughts. "Living out here, the owner should have a generator."

"Let's go," she said after checking out the window. "I

saw a chimney in the front of their house when we drove in. Worst-case scenario, we beg to stay inside their living room to keep warm. At these temperatures and with sleet, we'll freeze by morning if we don't regroup."

Jules grabbed their shoes and placed Toby's down in front of him. She worried about the evidence being damaged by the cold while in her trunk. It was still the safest place to store the metal box and Ziploc carton. They couldn't risk those items returning to Axel's hands. He would destroy evidence. Every single young woman represented in those Ziplocs deserved to be acknowledged. Their families deserved to be notified. It was the only way they would find any peace, considering Axel hadn't admitted to all his crimes. Some families might still be waiting up at night, waiting for news of a loved one.

After sliding into her runners, Jules laced them up and stood. Hands on her hips, she asked, "Ready?"

They had no idea who owned the home now or what kind of reception they would receive. Someone who'd kept Teddy's tradition alive with the shed couldn't be all bad. Or so she hoped.

"Let's roll," he said after pushing to standing.

"We should probably take the backpack with us," she wondered out loud.

"I can get it," he said.

Jules stopped him with a hand up. "I'll take this one, big guy."

Toby's mouth opened to protest, then clamped shut just as quickly. She wasn't being stubborn. She was being realistic. He needed to conserve energy. He offered a quick nod of concession.

She shouldered the backpack after removing the chair

wedged underneath the door handle. But first, she collected their weapons and placed them inside.

Toby led the way to the main house, where a light was on in the back room. Kitchen?

He must be right about the generator. Could they throw themselves on the homeowner's mercy? Ask to spend the rest of the night inside the home?

They could circle back to Jodie's house. She might let them stay there if push came to shove. Hopefully, it wouldn't come to driving on icy roads.

"You should do the knocking," Toby said, stepping aside as they reached the back porch.

Sleet that felt like needles against her skin came down in sheets. Ice had already built up on the concrete porch, causing Jules to slip and nearly bite it. She grabbed Toby's arm to steady herself and more of those rockets shot through her. That was one way to keep warm, she mused, trying to keep her mood light instead of panicking.

Mother Nature was the great equalizer. She didn't discriminate. Frostbite affected everyone equally. So did hypothermia. Cold was cold.

She shivered against the biting wind as she raised a fist to knock on the screen door. The wood door swung open before she had a chance to bring her knuckles down on the glass.

An older woman stood on the other side of the door. She had to be in her late sixties if she was a day. Her full head of gray hair was piled on top of her head in a bun. She had a kind but worn look, like she'd spent too many hours in the sun. She wore a thick flannel nightgown that fell past her ankles, revealing sheep-colored bootee slippers and a peek of wool socks. "I've been concerned about you two."

How did she know there were two of them? Did she watch the shed to see who came and went?

A glimmer of fear passed behind her eyes as she opened the screen door. "Please, come inside before you freeze to death standing out there."

Jules was already shivering from the frigid temps and needlelike sleet. Her body wanted to step inside the warmth despite warning bells going off in the back of her mind. She glanced to Toby, who hesitated.

Was he getting the same weird feeling that something was off?

Then the door opened wider, revealing a man standing next to the older woman with a gun pointed at her back.

Axel.

Chapter Twenty-Two

Jules's thoughts immediately snapped to the guns inside her backpack. Was there any way she could get to one of them without alerting Axel?

Coming face-to-face with the monster brought a cold chill down her spine that even an Amarillo ice storm couldn't beat.

Deciding against making a move that could cause Axel's trigger finger to twitch, killing an innocent person before he turned the weapon on them, Jules shifted her weight to hide the backpack behind her.

"Ms. Haven asked the two of you to come inside nicely," Axel said. "Now do as the kind lady said."

Toby stepped inside first as the pair backed away, keeping enough distance that he couldn't make a move for the gun. Axel had to realize they would never jeopardize an innocent civilian. Thus the hostage.

After her friend, Jules entered the kitchen. Toby intentionally placed his body in front of hers.

"Close the door," Axel demanded, shutting off their means of easy escape. He studied Jules for a long moment. "And set the backpack on the floor where I can see it."

Jules did as instructed, muttering a curse that only Toby

was close enough to hear. Setting Axel off while he had a gun in his hand would end in disaster.

"Kick it over to me," Axel commanded, clearly feeling in charge of the situation.

She did, biting her tongue. Staying calm and assessing the situation might just keep them alive. Without being obvious, Jules studied the room in search of anything that could be used as a makeshift weapon. She'd once used a glass flower vase on a restaurant table.

"I knew it was you the minute the story broke after I killed that bitch of a sister of yours," Axel said to Toby.

Toby's hands clenched into fists. Anger rolled off her friend in palpable waves.

Ms. Haven stood there as her five-foot-four-inch frame shook with fear. She mouthed an apology.

Jules gave a slight head shake. It broke her heart that the elderly woman blamed herself in any way for this nightmare. Ms. Haven didn't need to apologize for a monster's actions. None of what was happening was her fault. She was caught in the middle of something that had nothing to do with her. If anything, Jules should be the one to apologize. If she hadn't insisted they go searching for answers, Ms. Haven would be safe in her bed right now.

If there was a hell, there had to be a special place there for bottom-feeders who took advantage of the kindness of strangers. For jerks who used them and then tossed them in the trash like garbage. For monsters who wrecked so many lives by feeding their own twisted desires.

"You did this to me," Axel said, his gaze intent on Toby. "This is all your fault. All those women you made me kill. Their blood is on your hands."

It was taking all Toby's willpower not to make a move toward Axel. Jules could read her friend's intent in his tense body language and the way he clenched his jaw, the way his muscles corded and in the way he leaned forward ever so slightly, like a runner about to jump-start as soon as a whistle was blown.

"You're off base," Toby finally ground out.

"Really?" Axel's voice was higher pitched now, like he was working into a frenzy. "Are you trying to tell me that you weren't the one who turned your back on my brother at the pool? You aren't the one who let him drown? Because I stood there on the edge of the pool and watched every second of it."

Toby didn't immediately speak.

"You took him away from me," he said, his voice almost to hysterics. "He was the only one who ever cared, who took a beating so I wouldn't have to because I was bad."

"You weren't bad," Jules said as calmly as possible. "You were a kid."

"Bed wetters get a beating, my stepdad used to say," Axel continued.

There was something almost sympathetic about the man standing in front of them now. Like he'd transformed back to that little kid taking beatings right before their eyes. Jules had never met a criminal who didn't have a horrific story behind them. But not everyone who'd been beaten or abandoned took their pain out on innocent people. There was no excuse for the monster Axel had become.

"But my brother stood up for me," Axel continued, like he'd been wanting—no, *needing*—to unburden himself for years.

"This is your chance, Axel," she said. Using his name was a calculated move. He would either ramp up his hate or be calmed by it. She needed to figure out which way he would go since calming him down might save their lives. "Tell us what your stepdad did to you."

His eyes filled with fire and rage. For a split second, Jules thought her instincts were off and she'd just made a fatal mistake.

"He punished me just like I punish others," Axel bit out, spitting out the words.

"You're still alive," she pointed out. "Why did you kill your victims?"

He became indignant now. "I showed them mercy."

"How? By killing them?" she pressed. If Axel ended up with the upper hand, she deserved to know why he killed her.

"I ended it for them," he raged. "I'm merciful, not like that son of a bitch who hurt me. They don't have to wake up every day afraid I'll come back and hurt them all over again."

"Rape," she corrected. "Not hurt. You raped them. And then you took their lives in the most horrific way, watching them die by your hands. That's not mercy, Axel." Jules's brain was working overtime to figure out how to get Ms. Haven away from the monster and give them a fighting chance to take him down. He'd come out better after the chopper *accident*, if that story still held water, than all three of the other occupants. Had he known it would go down? Somehow anticipated the crash?

How was that possible?

"It ended for them right there," he argued. "They didn't have to deal with the pain that came after. The nightmares that haunt you."

"You were a child, Axel," she said. "You didn't deserve what happened to you."

He took in a sharp breath, expanding his chest until he

looked like the six-foot-two-inch man he'd become. His eyes glazed over like he was in some kind of trance. Bad signs.

"Bed wetters get a beating," he began chanting.

Ms. Haven slowly moved her hand behind her toward a drawer as she caught Jules's gaze.

No. Please. Don't do anything that could get you killed.

They needed time to figure out their next move.

"Bed wetters get a beating," the chant continued. Axel was working himself up. Was this his routine? How he worked himself up to rape and murder?

The man had decided he was freeing those he tortured by killing them. He built himself up to be a saint inside his own mind.

Between Ms. Haven taking matters into her own hands and the energy building inside Axel, any little misstep could cause his finger to twitch. One shot was all it would take to send a bullet through the older woman's heart.

She needed to figure out a way to stop this runaway train from accelerating.

Before Jules could think of a next move or a way to warn Ms. Haven to stop, the drawer slowly opened. Axel was so focused on chanting and staring the two of them down, he didn't seem to notice Ms. Haven's slow movements as she slipped her hand inside the drawer.

A moment later, she came out with a chopping knife.

Tension caused the muscles in Jules's shoulders to pull taut. At this rate, she feared they might snap. Not that it would matter. If Axel had his way, she'd be dead first.

She needed to think up a distraction.

"We found your metal box," she shouted at him, causing his gaze to refocus onto her. There was so much rage in his eyes she was almost knocked a step back when his gaze landed hard on her. "I sent it off to be analyzed. Soon enough, the whole world will know what you did and who you really are."

"That's not… It was… You did—"

"Yes, we did," she countered, trying to take control of the situation.

Toby reached back and squeezed her hand. Panic sent her pulse racing. He wanted her to keep going because he was about to make a move.

"THAT'S RIGHT," Jules continued, just like Toby hoped she would. He'd given her a signal, hoping she'd picked up on it.

So far, Toby had had to fight every instinct inside him that caused him to want to launch himself across the kitchen and dive into the bastard who had squeezed out too many innocent lives, including his sister's.

For five years, this man had taunted Toby. Axel had haunted Toby's dreams and caused him to relive the horrific details of his sister's rape and murder.

Staring the man down, Toby realized he'd allowed this bastard free rent in his head far too long. Lila was gone, and there was nothing Toby could do to bring his baby sister back, no matter how much it pained him to admit that he hadn't been there to protect her when she'd needed him most. He would take that knowledge to the grave.

The fact she fought back wasn't what killed her. In Axel's twisted world, he was releasing her from the pain he'd caused her—pain that would follow her the rest of her days. That bastard was going to kill her either way. He considered it mercy. It had nothing to do with the advice Toby had given her. Lila had lived long enough to tell law enforcement who'd killed her in her own way. And now the man stood in front of Toby.

The rage he'd felt in those first moments in the kitchen

was dissipating. Anger had kept him in his own mental prison far too long. It was time to let go, accept the fact his sister wasn't coming back and realize she would never have wanted him to live this way.

Lila would have asked Toby to forgive the bastard who'd murdered her. Not for Axel's sake but for Toby's. He could see that so clearly now.

The monster standing on the opposite side of the room had his own mental prison to live in. But he was going to jail for the rest of his life so he couldn't hurt another innocent soul. It was the best way to honor Lila.

Toby noted the knife Ms. Haven was currently trying to conceal. The long, sharp blade glinted from the side of her bony wrist. He practically willed her not to make a move.

"Your brother was a bully," Jules sounded off, causing Axel to shift the barrel of the gun to point at her.

Ms. Haven used the opportunity to spin around and then stab Axel. She'd reached for his chest, but he sidestepped in time to take the blade into his shoulder instead. For a split second, he stared at the blade that she jabbed farther inside him.

"Run!" Jules said to the elderly woman, drawing Axel's fury.

He fired the gun at the exact moment Toby pushed Jules out of the bullet's path. Instead of hitting her, it clipped him. He'd add it to the long list of injuries sustained in recent days and move the hell on.

Because Axel still had a weapon in his hand.

Toby dived toward the big guy, focusing on all the rage he'd had inside him over the last five years to cover the pain. He'd pay the piper later for that move. Right now, though, it worked.

He slammed into Axel's knees and heard a crack. A

groan followed as Jules managed to knock the gun out of Axel's hand. It went flying across the floor as Axel gripped the counter to brace himself.

Axel went down anyway, fighting as he slammed into the tile floor.

Toby rolled over, attempting to free his good hand, but Axel stopped him cold. The monster's knee came up, slamming into Toby's inner thigh. He released a grunt and tried to rally.

And then the snick of a bullet engaging in a chamber stopped them both.

Feet squared in an athletic stance, Jules stood just out of range with her weapon trained on Axel.

The monster froze, caught off guard by the turn of events.

Toby seized the moment, rolling out of grasp despite the pain to his right wrist.

"Hands where I can see 'em," Jules demanded as Toby caught his breath.

He managed to sit up, half expecting Axel to do the same.

Instead, the man looked dead straight at Jules.

"You're going to have to shoot," he said with a steady, even tone. Resigned? Ready to meet his maker?

Or was this a trick? A distraction from a monster who'd mastered the art?

Jules's hand was steady on her weapon.

"I'll shoot," she said, calm as you please. "But I'm not going to kill you. You don't deserve it." She rocked on her heels while maintaining sharp aim. "I'll shoot your right leg first and then your left, so you won't be able to run." There was a steadiness to her voice that said she meant business.

"You won't do it," Axel warned. "And if you tried, I'd move so you hit my heart."

"You won't be fast enough," Jules stated as Toby panted, trying to bring his breathing back to a reasonable pace.

As it was, he'd been nicked by a bullet and was bleeding.

It had taken all his energy to dive into the bastard. Toby had nothing left to give.

"You might as well do it now," Axel said, almost begging despite trying to cover it up.

"Or what?" Jules asked.

"I'll do it myself," Axel warned.

"No, you won't," Jules countered. "Do you know how I know?"

He didn't respond, just shot knives at her with his glare.

"Because you would have done it by now," she continued. "You're a coward who hurts innocent, unsuspecting people." She bit those last words out in a harsh tone. "You're not merciful. You're a monster."

He started toward her. The man was going to force her to shoot. Their training taught them to shoot to kill.

And then from behind, Ms. Haven sneaked back into the room without Axel realizing the older woman was coming toward him. She grabbed a cast-iron pan from on top of her stove and delivered a knockout blow.

Axel's gaze widened in surprise as his head snapped forward. He didn't have time to put his hands out before his head smacked the tile and he slumped over.

Ms. Haven stood over him. "Bastard made me miss my beauty sleep."

The snappy comment shouldn't have made Toby and Jules laugh as hard as it did. But it was over. Axel was going back to jail, where he belonged.

Toby had no energy left to get up as Jules went to work tying Axel's hands and feet behind his back and Ms. Haven tended to Toby's newest wound.

"Thank you," Jules said to the elderly woman, wrapping her in a hug as the sounds of vehicles pulling up outside caught their attention. As far as they knew, Axel worked alone.

Chapter Twenty-Three

Jules raced to the front window two steps behind Ms. Haven, needing to be prepared for whatever they were about to face.

"It's the cavalry," Ms. Haven said, sounding as confused as Jules felt.

"What the hell?" Jules asked before relaying the message loud enough for Toby to hear. "We have a deputy, an ambulance and a fire truck."

Ms. Haven opened the front door, ushering everyone inside as she rattled off her statement to the deputy.

"Officer down in the kitchen," Jules immediately said to an EMT. She did an about-face and bolted down the hall as he followed, hot on her heels.

By the time she got to Toby with help, he was unconscious.

She immediately dropped down beside him, cupping his face. "Don't leave me like this, Toby." Tears welled in her eyes, blurring her vision. "Please. You're my best friend, my love, the person I want to spend the rest of my life with. Stay with me." Tears streamed down her face.

"Ma'am" was all she heard as the EMT urged her to take a step back as he placed an oxygen mask over Toby's nose and mouth.

This was real. This was happening. Toby was in danger of slipping away.

"Please don't go," she whispered when she could get close enough to his ear again as another EMT started working on him. "I don't want to do this life without you. You're my world. You're everything to me. I love you, Toby. Do you hear that? I can finally admit it to myself, to you. I've been in love with you since I saw you at the coffee shop that day. You didn't belong to me then, but everything inside my heart says you belong to me now. Don't leave me alone now that I've finally realized how much I love you."

"I'm sorry," the EMT said, interrupting the moment to lift Toby onto a gurney.

"Can I come with you?" she asked.

"No, ma'am," the EMT said. "But you can follow us to the hospital in your own vehicle." He paused for a second. "I wouldn't recommend it on these roads, though."

All Jules could do was helplessly stand there in the kitchen as the man she loved was wheeled away from her, fighting for his life.

A second later, Ms. Haven was at her side, wrapping her in a hug. "You shouldn't drive right now."

"I have to," Jules said, doing her level best to stem the flood of tears staining her cheeks. "I have to know that Toby is going to live. He's my partner."

"That's it—you're coming with me," Ms. Haven said. The woman might be tiny, but she was tough as nails.

Jules must have looked at her like she had three foreheads.

"I have two coats and a snowmobile in the garage for when my grandson comes to visit," Ms. Haven said. "Let's go."

Jules wasted no time in following the elderly woman. Though, the word *elderly* didn't apply to this spunky senior. Before they left the kitchen, she stopped long enough to ask the deputy, "How did you know to come here?"

"My boss got a call from yours," the deputy said. "Said he got a series of texts from you."

"Keys to my trunk are in the backpack," Jules stated. "You'll find more evidence inside." She hesitated for a moment, dropping her gaze to a still-unconscious Axel. "He's slippery."

"I've been warned," the deputy said, pulling out the kind of restraints that reminded her of the ones used on Hannibal Lecter in *The Silence of the Lambs*. "Don't worry." He lifted one of the metal restraints. "I got this."

Axel would be locked up in similar fashion to the animal he turned out to be.

That was all Jules needed to know as Ms. Haven reached for her hand, clasped it in hers like a schoolgirl and led her to a closet where she kept snowsuits and helmets.

Once suited up, Ms. Haven brought the snowmobile around to pick Jules up on the front porch.

They got to the hospital less than a minute behind the ambulance.

"Go on," Ms. Haven urged. "I've got a lot to clean up back home."

Jules hugged the woman before bolting inside the glass double doors of the hospital. She immediately spotted an information desk, headed straight to it.

"I'm afraid you'll have to wait in the waiting room," a worker wearing a *Jeannie* name tag said from the visitor's desk.

"Not an option," Jules said. "I need to be in his room when he wakes up."

"It's policy, ma'am," Jeannie continued with a frown.

"Send your supervisor if you need to, but I'll check every room in this ER until I find my partner's," Jules stated, leaving no room for doubt. She might get into trouble for being insistent, but she refused to leave Toby alone.

Jeannie seemed to know when she'd lost a battle. "Go ahead, but don't say I told you that he's behind curtain seven in the ER." The middle-aged woman winked.

"Thank you," Jules said with as much gratitude in her voice as she could muster before racing to find Toby. The thought of him opening his eyes to find an empty room pushed her feet to move faster.

Curtain seven was easy enough to slip inside. Beeps and whoosh sounds filled the air, along with the low hum of voices. There was no real privacy in a place like this. The curtain being closed only gave the illusion they were alone. Feet scampered around, visible at the gap between the curtain and the sterile tile flooring.

Jules pulled the roller stool next to Toby. It had to be a good sign he'd been left in a room alone so quickly. Right?

Or was she grasping at straws, willing him to be okay?

She took his hand in hers, linking their fingers. He reacted to her touch with a twitch of his hand.

His eyes blinked open. "Hey."

"Toby," she managed to say through tears that were so ready to well up and fall. "Hey."

"He's..."

"Under arrest and not going anywhere but a lifetime of prison," she reassured him.

Toby nodded, exhaled. Really exhaled. It was almost like he released all his anger and hurt with the air from his lungs. "Good."

"Yes," she confirmed.

He turned his head toward her and studied her. "You're crying."

"I thought I lost you," she said.

He brought her hand up to his lips and feathered a kiss. "You couldn't."

She wasn't sure how deeply that comment ran, but she finally got her courage up and had to tell him the truth about how she felt about him. Because life was too short not to tell someone how special they were.

"I hope you mean that, Toby Ward," she started, finding the courage to keep going as she spoke. "Because I have something to say to you."

His forehead wrinkled, concerned.

Telling him exactly how she felt meant risking his friendship, but she couldn't hold back or lie to herself any longer.

"I never believed in love at first sight until I met you," she started. "Standing there in that coffee shop, I was hit with something so fast and hard that I could barely breathe." She paused as he studied her. *Keep going.* It was her turn to take in a fortifying breath. "And then I looked up, and you were gone. Just like that. I'd missed you. Which was strange, because from the moment I laid eyes on you, something told me that you were going to be special in my life."

He didn't speak, which she took as a bad sign.

But she was going all in, no matter what. Once he had all the information, he could decide how he wanted to move forward.

"I made a deal with myself right then and there that if I ever felt that way again about another soul, I wouldn't let him get away," she continued, feeling her heartbeat thunder inside her chest. She'd never felt so shaky before in her life. "Fast-forward to when I walked in the conference room and saw you sitting there." She compressed her lips at the sweet memory. "I forced myself to take the seat next to you so you'd have to talk to me. And then I chickened out because we were coworkers, and I had no idea if you felt the same way. I settled for friendship, and we became best friends." She drummed up a little more courage. Enough to keep going. "But recent events have forced me to reevaluate what I'm willing to accept. I should have told you from day one that I was crazy about you, Toby. But I didn't." She didn't dare meet his gaze while feeling so vulnerable. "And I'll regret that for the rest of my life because I've been in love with you from that first day." She paused as more tears filled her eyes. "It's okay if you don't feel the same way. I decided it's better to know one way or the other. This way, I know that I took the chance and risked it all because I finally found my person. I found the love of my life. I found home."

Tears spilled out of her eyes as she exhaled, steeling herself for the rejection she was certain would come.

"I'm not sure what you see in me, Jules," Toby started, letting go of her hand to bring his to her chin, forcing her to lift her gaze to meet his. "But I'm the luckiest damn man on earth. I've loved you from day one, and I agree on one thing." He hesitated. "We've spent way too long fighting our feelings for each other. You're the best thing that's ever happened to me. I'm so in love with you that it's hard to breathe when I first see your face every day. I love you and, more than anything, want to make a life together."

Jules couldn't hold back her smile at hearing those words.

"I never want to leave your side again," he said. "And when I'm strong enough to get out of this bed and down on one knee, I intend to ask you to do me the great honor of marrying me."

Jules climbed in bed with Toby, curling up against his body as he feathered kisses on her face before finding her lips.

"Yes," she said when they finally pulled back. "In case you were wondering, my answer will be yes."

"Then let's not waste any more time," he said. "Marry me."

Jules couldn't hold back her smile. "Wild horses couldn't stop me from marrying you, Toby Ward."

She'd found the man she wanted to spend the rest of her life with, and as soon as he was cleared to leave the hospital, it was time to take him home to Mesa Point to meet the rest of her family—a family that would welcome him with open arms.

And she couldn't wait to bring him home.

* * * * *

Harlequin® Reader Service

Enjoyed your book?

Try the perfect subscription for Romance readers and get more great books like this delivered right to your door.

See why over 10+ million readers have tried Harlequin Reader Service.

Start with a Free Welcome Collection with free books and a gift—valued over $20.

Choose any series in print or ebook. See website for details and order today:

TryReaderService.com/subscriptions